Pe

Bre
Gl

'Never come back,' the other man said. He slammed the door on me. 'Forget England.'

Dad had promised to return for fourteen-year-old Darren and his sister Sally when he'd been taken away by the Army. But when the West Midlands area is evacuated before the Russians drop their germ bomb, he still hasn't returned and they are left behind. Only when Sally dies does Darren discover that the Affected Zone is being fenced in and that there is no escape for him or the small number of others immune to the disease.

With loneliness gnawing at him, Darren tries to re-establish his friendship with Alex. But Alex has teamed up with Budge, a vicious gangleader, and they both want Darren dead. However, worse than the struggle to survive alone against murderous gangs, hunger and fear, is the bitterness and anger he has to live with. Why did Dad betray his promise to return for them and leave them to their fates – Dad whom he had hero-worshipped?

Breaking Glass is a powerful and totally convincing story of one person's struggle to survive in a bleak and hostile world.

Brian Morse is a primary school teacher who lives in Warley in the West Midlands. He has previously published three novels as well as writing ghost stories for various anthologies.

BRIAN MORSE

Breaking Glass

Penguin Books

Penguin Books Ltd, 27 Wrights Lane, London W8 5TZ (Publishing and Editorial)
and Harmondsworth, Middlesex, England (Distribution and Warehouse)
Viking Penguin Inc., 40 West 23rd Street, New York, New York 10010, USA
Penguin Books Australia Ltd, Ringwood, Victoria, Australia
Penguin Books Canada Ltd, 2801 John Street, Markham, Ontario, Canada L3R 1B4
Penguin Books (NZ) Ltd, 182–190 Wairau Road, Auckland 10, New Zealand

First published by Lutterworth Press 1986
Published in Penguin Books 1988

Printed and bound in Great Britain by
Cox & Wyman Ltd, Reading

For Daniel

A bursary from the West Midlands Arts made possible
the writing of the initial draft of this novel.

PART ONE

Anna

This morning a fox by the hedge, at the bottom of Home Field. A thin, cautious, ragged, hungry fox.

A fox. How did it get here? How did it evade the guards, guns, mines, searchlights, electric current?

Beside me, Darren raises his glasses with swift stealth. I fear for the fox. I watch Darren instead. Amazement floods his face: no animals survived the war, an impassable fence rings the Midlands, the Forbidden Territory, no one in – no one out, the ground itself is poisonous. Then hope: if this survives, wherever it comes from, however it got here, it must prey on something, other life. Other life! One day our animal-less farm may hold animals ... Then hate floods his face.

I look away, watch the fox, brace myself for the inevitable shot. It seems a dream so sad.

"Poor fox. If we started farming he wouldn't be very popular," I say meantime.

"I'd have to go to the Fence, beg for stock, hope the Tripartite Committee's in a positive mood," Darren says tensely.

I hold my breath. Darren hates their computer terminal Communication Centres. Humiliation Centres he calls them.

"Stock?" I say. "You mean for the farm?" He doesn't answer. "Ask *them*? About starting a farm?"

"The glasses. Have them. Look," Darren says, "before it's gone." His voice is angry. "Have them, Anna."

I watch the fox slip away through the hedge. Then I focus the glasses instead beyond, past the fallen roofs, collapsing walls and broken glass of the dead Black Country towns, on the ten-metre fence ten miles away that strides along the M6. It has watchtowers every hundred yards, guards in masks and protective clothing, guns cocked, grenades ready, mortars primed. We are the carriers of a fatal disease.

"Will you go?" I insist. "The animals, Darren! Please make up your mind. Will you ask them?"

Seventeen years ago the Red Army occupied Western Europe. They and the Americans fought a five-day nuclear war over northern Germany. After the GIs had gone home an eastern triangle of England became the British People's Homeland, its governor Russian. Five years later the British Government demanded back the lost counties, broke off relations and staged border incidents. The Red Army invaded. The British Army launched its few missiles at Moscow, Prague and Warsaw. The Russians responded with a germ bomb over Leicester.

We walk back to our hill-top home, through two fields, along the lane. Where we live looks out north to Birmingham, west to Wales, south into Worcestershire. When we came here first we found an old sales brochure – "desirable property, £150,000 or nearest offer".

I try to talk.

"Shall I go instead?" I ask. "The car's like a tank. I'll be safe. I'll keep an eye out. I can handle a gun. You know that. It was I taught you to shoot."

Every time he goes down there it could be the last time. I never expect him to return. Not all the prisoners in this cage seek peace like us.

"I'll go, I'll go," he says as though it were inevitable. But for seconds his finger had itched as he sighted my fox. Yes, it was my fox, mine. "Damn your fox, your Miraculous Mr Fox."

"There must be more to life than staying alive," I say in defence. "Think of it – new life! Not just us. Lambs, chicks – "

He's going for me, not for himself. I know it. I ought to be moved.

"I've left you something," he says as we reach the door. "Something I want you to read. The beginning of an explanation."

"Of the war?" I ask. "Of our predicament?"

I'm awkward because I know exactly what it is.

"No, just of me," he says. "I only know about me."

He goes in, sure of that.

His memoirs, Darren's memoirs.

Darren

The weather's warm but the car engine's three months cold. It hisses and rattles. A loose bodywork panel vibrates. The suspension creaks.

At the bend I don't bother to look back, not even a glance in the mirror. I don't suppose she's watching anyway, more likely in the house, deep in a book or one of her poems. We're cold fish, Anna and I.

Reluctantly I think of the fox. My first impulse was to kill it. Raise my gun – I always carry it. Obliterate. Then I saw Anna's face. Her face held an expression I'd never seen before: so tender.

The road goes down precipitously. Probably it was never well kept up, even in the pre-war days. In the winter it's a stream. I aim the car roughly down it, my foot tight on the brake. The pot-holes and cracks and rackety steering conspire to take me precisely where I want, off the hill and into the crease of countryside before the town. Here I proceed with great caution. A tree that fell in winter storms three years ago caused me months of labour to hack and saw away. I gave up sawing when the car just squeezed through. I hold my breath as I edge past. The old engine spits.

This is a hopeless enterprise I am embarked upon. That fox was a fluke, a chance in billions, a mangy ragged creature.

A farm – this is foolishness. Nothing can survive. Nothing has so far. Only us, a couple of thousand human freaks; snakes; some birds; and the insects. The idea that the Tripartite Committee will agree to our request is sheer lunacy. Fresh milk and eggs for us, fresh meat – why should they give us the opportunity of that pleasure, even if it were possible? Unless they're experimenting again. There are rumours the kind of bomb they dropped on us has become acceptable to their way of thinking, like the nuclear bomb before it. In which case they'll be needing data. They probably shoved the fox over the fence themselves.

Now the beginning of the West Midlands town looms above me, a row of estates precisely on the line of the Green Belt, hanging over it, greedily lapping up the greenness. I drive the wrong way up a dual carriageway. There's a gaping hole on the other side. I remember the mystery explosion that made it. We slept outside that night, fearing our house would be raided.

This close to the town it becomes more difficult to breathe. My anguish increases. There are ghosts there in these back streets; I go there as little as possible – Sally, my dead sister – Dad: he left us behind – Alex, who should have been my friend but was my enemy – Budge, who *was* my enemy, and was true to form. Deaths and betrayals.

Every time I come down here I give Anna the key to the drawer in the bureau where I keep my "memoirs", telling her if I don't come back, read it. Probably she read it long ago, even if she's never told me. On the other hand, perhaps she's never touched it and never means to.

Nothing new here except coarse grass ever higher, mangling the tarmac. My car leaves tracks through it. I watch them in my mirror. I hardly realise I've reached the round-about until my front wheels hit a kerb and I'm thrown off course. I'm on the central island. With difficulty I extricate the car. I turn down into Hasbury. Blackheath and Old Hill unfold to my gaze, all the dead towns.

PART TWO

Darren's Memoirs

1

To begin somewhere, like the stories they made us write at primary school, subject on the board: 'My Summer Holiday', 'My Family', 'Lost on a Desert Island'. What panic that used to cause! So much to write, but where to start? 'Use your *imagination*,' they used to say. 'Where's your imagination?' But where to start? So many details. The time? The place? The weather? What's it all really about?

Primary school, which I hated, secondary school which I hated even more than primary – the bus shelter opposite the school, I'll start there.

'The Day The War Started'.

I stood so many times at that bus stop, in that bus shelter, the weather details blur into one. It was always too hot or too cold.

Which was it that day?

No, wait! I can work it out. Two hours later I was lying on my back, stunned by the butt of a gun, Mrs Homer our neighbour screaming a few feet from me. All I could focus on was the sky which rolled and rolled around me.

It was weakly sunny, mixed grey and white clouds scudding. An average English day.

Fool that I am, it was precisely those conditions that aided the spread of the disease caused by the germ bomb. How could I forget?

As I stood and waited for the bus I didn't know that the war would start that day. But there was a dull ache of hopelessness in me, a fat boy at a bus stop – for I was fat then and self-conscious with it.

I stared alternately at the school across the way and up the street. Usually the 242 came every half an hour. Today it didn't. It was an hour before it appeared, and I was the only one waiting. What I could have done in that hour, now I look back. Would I have got it done though?

Every time I shifted position my feet crunched fragments of glass. Someone had smashed up the shelter. That happened often. The wonder was they ever bothered to mend it. Even before the war the whole area needed a vast sweep-up. Yet they found money for their armies, and planes and bombs and experiments.

School was strangely deserted that day: a dozen teachers and a hundred children out of the usual thousand. As the day wore on more of us disappeared. Cars arrived groaning with roof-racks, trailers attached, caravans swaying. Teachers went as well as pupils. There was no Head after dinner.

I listened to the roar of engines, revving a little closer to safety, away from Them, the Reds, the Invaders. I sat and thought bitterly: Dad could have laid his hands on a car somewhere. He can drive. I could drive at a pinch.

I called into Mrs Herbert's office before leaving school. Mrs Herbert was my favourite teacher, but she'd gone, in a hurry to judge by the top of her usually tidy desk. This made me know Dad and Sally and I had to go too.

I was the only one at the bus stop, the last one home from school.

"Have to walk?"

"A bus came eventually." My bag went under the kitchen table. "The roads are jam-packed. At this rate we'll be the only ones left, Dad."

"They say on the radio, councils are moving people out," he said.

"We *are* going?" I felt very insistent.

Dad made a face. "Much as I dislike the idea of finishing up in a refugee camp, yes we'll go. Better dead than red they say. I'm not sure. But you know that." He turned up the radio. It was on his knees. "Listen. They've been promising this all afternoon."

"We have reason to believe that within twenty-four hours the Red Army intends to launch a further invasion from the so-called British People's Homeland," the Prime Minister was saying. The familiar voice sounded feverish, out of control.

"During the last hour the commander of the Red Army has issued a series of demands concerning our nuclear weapons. Needless to say we cannot give in to these demands and stay a free people. Accordingly I have given the enemy to understand we will fight if provoked. Several border incidents have already occurred in the Watford area."

"How can we fight them without using nuclear weapons ourselves, Dad?" I burst in.

"We have guns, planes, tanks, rockets," Dad said severely. "God knows they're enough. If they don't use nuclear weapons we have no need to either, and I don't think they will. They've seen more of the horror of it all than us. Most of Germany's cordoned off, remember; that lost them lots of political popularity."

"I appeal to the British people to stay calm," the voice on the radio continued. "Stay at home. Leave the roads clear for the Army. The civilian population will be evacuated in an orderly fashion by local councils."

Dad turned off the radio. "More people from the Midlands have set off than are left, they say." He put the radio aside with a sigh. "Go and see where your sister is, Darren. She's got to understand she mustn't go too far from the house. I suppose these coaches are going to arrive sooner or later."

I ran out of the house. I was full of relief. I didn't want to stay and wait for the Red Army. Everyone with any sense knew they weren't the devils propaganda made them out to be, yet there had been reported atrocities five years before.

I pulled up, panting, by the hedge at the bottom of the lawn. Below me was the park. At the bottom of the two-hundred-metre slope ran a stream; on its other side was a small wood. Through the trees you glimpsed a road. It wasn't a very important one, mainly used in the mornings and evenings as a short-cut by local people. Tonight it was very busy.

"Sally!" I called.

A movement in the next-door garden made me turn. But it wasn't Sally. It was Mrs Homer trying to slip back into her house without being seen.

"That sister of yours gone missing again?" she said quickly.

I could see she felt guilty, why she ought to feel guilty. It was because of their car out on the front ready to evacuate them, its back seat full of *things*, useless objects that would be of no use to them where they were going, hairdriers and irons and electric toasters, when there could have been a space for me and Sally and Dad.

She gabbled on. "A right wanderer she is. Always has been. Do you remember that time ... " She stopped. She was no great admirer of Sally's though she liked me all right. "Packed, have you?" she asked.

"Dad's only just made up his mind to go," I said.

"Jack reckons we're best out of here as soon as possible. We've hung on long enough," Mrs Homer said. "They can't be stopped and no one can guarantee there won't be fighting here, whatever any government says. We know this little place near Ffestiniog. A pity you haven't a car – "

"If we were so lucky," I said meaningfully.

"You ought to start packing all the same," Mrs Homer said.

She began to go back in. "You see to it, Darren. You don't want to get left. The council are sending coaches round, Jack says."

I wished I could tell her what I thought of her. At least they could have offered to take Sally. She wouldn't have taken up much space.

I got over the hedge and ran down the bank. My eight-year-old sister had a hideaway down by the stream. I'd used it myself when I was her age. I ran along the stream bank to where it was narrow enough to jump comfortably. The rope was hanging down where it had always been, still threatening to break where it had frayed. Was it the same one? I suppose it had to be. "Stay where you are or I'll undo it!" Sally hissed as I began to clamber up. "Here's private."

"You've got to come home," I called. "Dad says so. It's going to be dangerous. We're leaving."

"Dangerous? He said it would be all right when they sent us home from school this morning."

"There might be fighting."

"Here?" Sally said in a scornful way. She was going through a know-all phase. "Here's not important. Who'd want to fight here?"

"It's what Dad says, not me. We've got to get ready for a coach. It'll be coming for us. The council's sending it."

"There's an awful lot of cars on the road," Sally observed.

"There was earlier. Come on."

"There are even more now."

"Let me up to see," I called, tempted.

"Okay."

I began to climb.

"If it will hold your weight," she added maliciously.

I shimmied up the rope on to the platform. "Watch it," I said, but not really minding. My sister was a pretty girl – everyone said so. I even grudgingly admitted it myself. Having no Mum had made us grow up close together. "You've made a good job of this," I said to please her for she seemed

in a touchy mood. Then I gasped at how right she was about
the road. Where it bent back on itself like a flexed elbow over
the bridge the traffic was bumper to bumper. And everything
was going the same way.

"It's like on holiday," Sally said excitedly. "See, there's
three caravans in a row. Some are pulling little trailers. Is that
a washing-machine on that roof-rack?"

"The Homers aren't the only ones to have the idea then,"
I said, remembering the purpose behind it all.

"What idea?"

"What I told you! The Red Army's coming. Everyone's
heading for Wales. Let's go back to the house straightaway.
I don't want Dad to change his mind."

As we stepped into our garden there was a scream from the
front of the house. Then I heard Dad's voice too, raised in
uncharacteristic anger.

"Stay here!" I pushed Sally back. "Don't you move!" I
ran as fast as I could up the side of the house.

There was a lorry in our cul-de-sac, its back wide open.
Two men with guns were in the road by the doors. A huddle
of figures was cowering inside. The men with the guns swung
towards me. They were wearing dark green uniforms I'd never
seen before, some form of Home Guard or Citizens' Army.
"Watch out!" one of them called. They were British, not
Russian. That was no comfort if they knew Dad's views. That
was my first thought: revenge. Take advantage of the
confusion to settle old scores. He'd been quite well known.

I rushed at the two men pulling Dad away.

"Stay back, Darren!" Dad shouted. "I'll come back. Don't
worry. I'll come back for you. It's all right."

"No you don't, you little bugger!" shouted a man keep-
ing Mrs Homer at bay as I tugged at Dad's captors. He swung
the butt of his gun against my head. I fell to the ground.

The men dragged Dad and Mr Homer into the road. They
threw them into the back of the lorry and slammed the
doors. There were shouts from inside. The man covering

Mrs Homer jumped on to the running-board as the lorry backed out of the cul-de-sac. The sky spun round me.

2

Next morning was grey. We'd got up early. There was a massive breakfast – bacon, sausages, eggs, tomatoes, fried bread, everything Mrs Homer had in the fridge. She'd taken us in. Sally just pushed her plate away while I wolfed mine down: I'd been incapable of eating last night. Mrs Homer sipped at a cup of tea and puffed at a cigarette. I'd never seen her smoke before. Mr Homer had smoked like a chimney, with her chasing round after the ash.

We watched the news on an extra early Breakfast TV special. Fighting had already started. It had been going on since yesterday evening, not only in and around London but beyond into Bedfordshire, Berkshire and Buckingham. Clashes were reported even beyond there. London was now deserted and part of it on fire. The government appealed to the country to stay calm. The traffic clogging the roads was impeding military operations. Authorised vehicles only. Orders to shoot on sight. Looters executed. The rumour that someone had shot at the Prime Minister was a propaganda lie. However, certain CND dissidents had been arrested and would be tried at a later date. The government reserved its right to use nuclear weapons, though – of course – only if attacked first. It might have been another place, this country England.

"It's ridiculous to expect people to stay put with a war coming in their direction." Mrs Homer clicked her tongue. I wished she would stay, but a murmur of traffic from the road below told you how many agreed with her.

Suddenly the lights and TV went off. "A sign." Outside there was a sudden brightness in the sky. "Hardly worth lighting the candles. I'll wash up." Mrs Homer busied herself at the sink while Sally and I sat at the table staring at each other. I couldn't fathom Sally's look. She hadn't smiled or spoken since last night.

"We'll pin a card on your back door – no, put one on your kitchen table. No use advertising you're away," Mrs Homer said. "I'll leave directions for your Dad as to how to get to Ffestiniog and the place where we'll be. He'll be all right then, won't he?"

Sally looked away from me, at Mrs Homer. She stood up. "Why did they take Dad?" she asked.

"I told you already, dear," Mrs Homer said patiently. Now she was on her own she couldn't do enough for us, explain enough of what she understood, invent where she didn't. Was it because she was scared of travelling all that way on her own? She hadn't invited us to come yesterday afternoon. Or was I just being cynical when I ought to be grateful? I hung my head, waiting for the two to argue.

"Dad hadn't done anything."

"No more had my husband." Mrs Homer was suddenly on her guard.

"Then why?"

"They were some kind of special army group. They were short of men. It wasn't because they'd done anything wrong."

"Dad wouldn't shoot anyone. He doesn't believe in fighting. He told me so. He was – what's the word, Darren? Darren!"

"A pacifist." I raised my head.

"I told you, dear. Not for fighting but as labourers, for

20

fetching and carrying and digging trenches, all those things they do in wars. That's what they wanted them for, just like the press-gangs years ago. And this cul-de-sac was just their cup of tea. There were your dad and my husband out chatting in the front and no one else to see what was happening or to stop them.'' She began methodically putting away the crockery she'd dried. ''No more talk that way, please, Sally. I don't think I can stand it.'' She took the rubbish bin outside. Then beneath our gaze – she made us check with her – she went round all the windows, turning off the gas, electricity and water. ''Well,'' she said. ''Really time to go now, I think.''

I carried our two cases out into the early morning sun and waited by the car. Mrs Homer brought Sally out by the hand and locked the front door. The rumble of the cars on the road below seemed the most terrible noise to me.

''Who'd have thought it would come to this?'' Mrs Homer said, her voice very loud in the morning air. ''God – I think I'm going to cry after all. I've got this feeling I'll never see here again.''

Sally came and stood close to me. ''Dad said we were to wait. He said he was coming back. I heard him. I'm not going.''

''Don't be daft,'' I said. I had a job to control my voice. ''Don't be soft. He'll know where we are. If we stay, who'd look after us?''

''We can look after ourselves. You can look after me. You're old enough. I'm not going,'' Sally said.

I tried to take her hand, but she backed away as if I was contagious.

Mrs Homer was unlocking the car. ''What's the matter, Sally, dear?'' she asked. She had a way of addressing you as 'dear' that had always irritated me. I guess it irritated Sally too.

''I'm not going!'' Sally shouted. ''I'm waiting for Dad. He told us to wait. You were there. You've no right taking us away.''

"Now, Sally, look," Mrs Homer said. "I've put off leaving in order to take you. Darren wasn't well enough to travel last night. But it might mean all the difference between life and death to me. And your dad wouldn't mind me taking you. He'd want it. He'll know where you've gone."

Sally ran off across the front gardens and round the corner of our house. I stared after her.

"Don't stand there. Fetch her, Darren!" Mrs Homer snapped. "Quickly."

I ran round the corner of the house and down the side. Sally was trying the back door.

"It's locked," I said, wrenching at her arm. "I've got the key."

She flared at me. "I'm not coming! *You* go! Leave me the key."

"No, look here – "

"I want Dad." She was beyond tears, in a hysterical temper.

"We've got to be sensible – "

Mrs Homer came round the corner of the house. "Grab her!" she shouted at me.

That did it. Sally gave us both a look of withering contempt, ran down the garden and jumped over the hedge. I stared after her in disbelief.

"The ungrateful little bitch!" Mrs Homer screamed. "Fetch her, Darren. Run! I can't wait much longer. I can't." It was a job to tell for whom she was most desperate. I must have stood staring. "*Run!*"

What if Sally's right? I thought as I raced after her. The thought had occurred to me as well. But hadn't Dad shouted he was coming back just to reassure us that no harm would come to him? Hadn't it really meant nothing? Wouldn't he be telling us to go if he were here now? I put on a spurt that took me much closer to Sally. She heard me behind her and ran faster too. She began to get away. I'd never been much good at running. "*Run!*" I heard Mrs Homer scream again.

We were right out in the middle of the park now and at

last I began to catch Sally up. She was stumbling along, strength fading. I called out to her. Her response was to try to break into a last run. Failing, she veered off towards the stream.

She flopped down beside it. I stood behind her, gasping. She gathered a handful of small stones and began to lob them one by one into the water, then chucked the whole lot in. I sat down beside her and watched the ripples and the final explosion.

"I'm not going, you know," she said after a couple of minutes. "I don't care what you do to me."

"Obviously," I said. I felt glad in a way. A difficult decision had been taken out of my hands.

Back at the house we found the car had gone. Mrs Homer had left our cases on the drive. Sellotaped to one was the card she'd written for Dad. I pocketed it. There was also a duplicate of our back door key. I suppose – though I'd not known it – that Dad had entrusted her with one some time in the past. I was relieved she'd gone. I couldn't have faced her.

I unlocked our back door and looked in every room. The house seemed really lonely and empty without Dad resting on the settee or bed.

I brought the radio into the kitchen and Sally and I sat with it between us. The Red Army was in Oxfordshire and wheeling north. The announcer (he said he was speaking from Bristol) described the chaos on the roads as unbelievable. Many people were stranded because they'd run out of petrol and, of course, most filling stations were closed. Those still open were doubling and redoubling their prices. The government had declared this illegal, and threatened fines after the war, but it wasn't making any difference.

I turned the radio off to save the batteries. I hadn't any money to replace them. I leant on my elbows and gazed at Sally. Had we done the right thing? Sally was only eight to my fourteen. Oughtn't I to have been taking the decisions?

"Well, what now?" she said. She seemed remarkably calm.

"We ought to go and have a look around the rest of the estate."

"I'll wait for Dad."

"You don't mind if I go?"

She shook her head, not worried at all.

I locked up carefully, after making sure Sally knew how to get out in an emergency. On the pavement I stood and looked at the other two houses across the road. Their cars had gone.

I began to have terrible doubts. If everyone else had gone or was going, why should we be different? I'd been persuading Dad to hurry up a few minutes before the soldiers had come.

I hurried up into the estate, up Keats Avenue, the wide road that ran right through it. I met only a few people in the road and saw only one car moving. There was no one I knew to speak to. Where Keats Avenue crossed Byron Road in the centre of the estate was a row of shops. Only the newsagent's was open.

After a minute of staring unseeingly at my own reflection in the window I dug deep into my pockets to find some money to buy sweets and went in. The owner took next to no notice of me. He was listening to the radio. The only papers were yesterday's. I stared at his rack of magazines. His wife came through from the back.

"No use hanging about here, Frank," she said. "Get locked up."

"I don't like to leave it," Frank said unhappily.

"Come on," she said. "Board up. There's no one to sell to."

"And leave all our stock?"

"And wait till they start dropping things? What's more important? I'll help you." She noticed me. "Haven't you somewhere to go?" she snapped.

I went without my sweets. The estate was so quiet that even here, in the middle, I could hear the traffic on the road below our house. I was drawn to it. I took short-cuts through the side-roads and found I'd not seen the last of Mrs Homer. Her car was only fifty metres from the turning out of the estate. In front of her were two double-deckers painted in a livery I didn't recognise. There were lorries full of people and possessions. Every thirty seconds or so the line moved on a few more yards. The drivers' faces were grim.

I went back into the estate, hoping Mrs Homer hadn't seen me. There must be someone I knew around still. I knocked on John Reed's door. I waited ages and hammered, but no one came. The same happened with Peter Shakespeare and Peter Bodeman and Daniel Trueman. A few people were still at home but they were all old. A mini laden with luggage and three children in the back seat, all younger than Sally passed me. They waved as if they were going on a great adventure – which I suppose they were. Then I turned a corner and twenty metres away from me a gang of five or six lads was coming in my direction. I faltered then walked on. They'd seen me. You don't turn your back on gangs.

I didn't recognise them at first. Then I stopped dead. One was Alex. He had been my best friend but over the two or three years since primary school we'd lost contact with each other. It was ages since we'd deliberately met up. I'd even heard he'd started going out seriously with girls, which I certainly hadn't. Nor had I found a friend as close as him.

I went forward. "Alex!" I called, a big artificial smile on my face. He and I had never quarrelled but it had become increasingly difficult to find things to say to him. And now he was with a gang.

One of the other faces snapped into focus. It was the classic situation – meeting your best friend with the person you least want to see.

"Budge!" I said faintly. If only I could have run. That great puffy-cheeked face with its perpetual mocking smile. My worst enemy – my only enemy.

"Hi, Fatso!" he said. "Where you waddling?"

I stepped into the gutter and tried to pretend I wasn't

concerned, that it was all water off the duck's back. Budge had other ideas. He jumped out into the road in front of me.

"Fatso, I said *where*!"

"Just home," I said as casually as possible. I tried to walk round him, but he stepped to one side to block me. Though I wasn't short he seemed to tower over me. He pushed his face down into mine. His eyes had always seemed too close together. He'd nicked himself shaving. And he was grinning. But Budge always grinned. He'd probably die grinning.

"Not so fast," he said. "I don't suppose your dad's lying in wait this time."

"I don't suppose he is," I said. (Last time Budge had victimised me, Dad had had to step in.) I looked aside at Alex. He was looking the other way.

"Knew him, didn't you?" Budge said to Alex, realising where my eyes had gone. "Before he got even fatter and more disgusting." Alex looked at me without expression. At least he didn't join in.

Budge pushed his face up against mine.

"One day I'll kill you, Fatso!" he said. "I swear I will. You disgust me. I hope the Reds get you."

I walked on, guessing the worst was over. He shoved me in the small of the back, but I didn't turn or even rub the place where he'd hit me. Don't answer back. Turn the other cheek. Ignore remarks. That was the strategy I employed when fat was the issue. But it didn't work with some people.

I thought of Alex. What was he doing with a cretin like Budge? I'd hero-worshipped Alex when I was ten. I'd always assumed he was still marvellous, just got different interests and I felt ashamed at times of not coming up to his standards.

I turned round at the corner and looked back.

The gang had gone, no Alex coming after me. It affected me, this glimpse of a long-lost friend, rather more than Budge's shove in the back.

3

Back home I crept upstairs. Sally was asleep on Dad's bed. I left her and sat in the kitchen. I turned on the radio. I was taut after my encounter on the street.

"Co-operate with the invader if necessary, otherwise avoid him," the announcer was saying, as if the Red Army was a form of acute disease. "Leave resistance to the Army. Keep off the roads." There was no mention of where the Red Army had got to. I fetched Dad's road atlas from the front room and tried to work out where they'd said the fighting had been this morning. It seemed to have got quite close to us, though Dad had always said it would peter out before it did, that they'd cobble out a solution. I also searched the map of Wales for Ffestiniog.

Then I looked at some old magazines and comics, but all the time I was listening for Dad's footsteps on the path outside. It had been a promise to come back, hadn't it? So he'd come. If he could. If he hadn't been caught up in the fighting and captured. Or killed. Or maybe, if he'd got away, he would have headed straight for a safe area expecting us to go with Mrs Homer or be carted away by the council. The permutations were endless, but some were more terrifying than others.

About half-past two Sally came down, sleep still in her eyes. She looked for Dad, saw he wasn't there. I had the radio on. It was saying the same things as earlier. She sat down and listened intently.

"Dad's in the army. Does that mean he'll get killed?" she asked suddenly.

"He won't be fighting," I said shortly. I was feeling mad with her. What had she dragged me into? "He's been forced to work for them." I didn't really know whether what Mrs Homer had said had been true. I'd gathered her husband and Dad had talked to the soldiers for a couple of minutes before they'd been dragged off. I thought that if Dad had gone on about banning the bomb and passive resistance they'd probably have shot him on the spot. So perhaps she'd been right.

I told Sally about Mrs Homer in the queue of traffic.

"I bet we could still catch her up," I said. "The traffic was moving so slowly I bet she's only gone a couple of miles."

"No, we decided," Sally said.

"You did."

"You could have made me go."

I wondered if that was true!

The electricity was still going. I cooked some baked beans, fried some bacon and buttered some bread. The only thing Sally said was that she wanted a drink of milk. I went to the front door. The milkman hadn't come. I hadn't thought of that. Our silence went on into the afternoon, broken only by the sound of the cars below. The traffic continued all afternoon. It wasn't a sound you could ignore. More than once the sound of arguments and fights and the demented tooting of horns came up to us. We didn't go down to see what it was all about.

I told Sally about having seen Alex, but she didn't remember him properly. It felt important I'd seen him, but not important in a way I could easily explain. But then Alex had probably left by now. His parents weren't the types to get caught out: two smart people with good jobs, though Alex had never seemed that fond of them. Anyway, Alex and Budge – that would rather have excluded me.

Sally kept asking for a drink of milk. She asked so often I felt like hitting her, it grated on my nerves so much. With all that was happening it was that silly little thing, the fact the Unigate man hadn't come and wouldn't come again till everyone came back and things returned to normal, that got through to me.

I tried to turn on the TV. There might have been a cartoon to keep Sally's mind employed, but the electricity was off by now. "I want someone to play with," Sally whined. She took decisions, like an adult, then acted like a baby.

The radio said, "The Red Army is now entering the East Midlands. In the south it has called a halt to its advance. Unofficially there is talk of a ceasefire and the redrawing of the boundaries of the British People's Homeland. The Red Army has announced its capture of seventeen of the twenty ex-American missile sites. Fierce fighting is reported to be going on for the remaining three, all in the north."

That seemed hopeful, but down on the road the traffic still hadn't slackened. No one was turning back.

"One day I'll kill you, Fatso!" Budge's way of expressing himself hadn't changed, nor had the menace of his threats. What if he found out Sally and I were on our own? I tried to brush aside such childish fears, but they were too real. How strange that one word could bring them all back – 'Fatso'. I looked at myself in the mirror. It seemed to me that I was less fat than I used to be, but I wasn't fool enough to believe that that would make any difference to someone like Budge. It was my character he was after, my *self*.

Later in the evening we went out and stood by the hedge at the end of the lawn and watched through the trees. I'd never imagined there were so many cars or so many people to fill them. On and on they went.

"The phone's ringing in the Homers'," Sally said suddenly.

We stepped over into Mrs Homer's back garden and walked carefully, like trespassers, to her back window and stared in. The phone, which stood on a little table in the back room, rang and rang.

"I bet it's Mr Homer," I said. "It's most likely him."

"It could be Dad," Sally suggested.

The phone stopped ringing.

"Why did you say that?" I cried.

Sally began to snivel.

Then it started ringing again.

I rattled the back handle – stupidly, because we'd been in the house when it had been locked and bolted. I kicked the door. If I broke the little pane of glass at the top could I undo the Yale? I would have smashed it except I realised that I'd never reach the bolt at the bottom.

Sally had stopped crying. She stared at me, wide-eyed. "It's Dad! I know it is!" she shouted. "Darren! Do something!"

"Like what?"

Sally had no scruples. She grabbed a stone from Mrs Homer's rockery and shattered the back room window. "Sally!" I gasped. She was trying to climb in now. I pulled her back and with another stone cleared away as many jagged pieces of glass as possible. Then I climbed into the room myself and ran towards the phone.

When I lifted it a voice said, very relieved, "That you, Sue? Thank God. I thought you might have left."

Mr Homer's voice.

"This is Darren from next door," I said. "Do you want your wife?"

Utter suspicion. "Darren? What are you doing there? Where is she? What's wrong? What's happened?"

"She drove off in the car, to Wales. This morning."

There was a brief silence in which I was afraid he'd ring off, so I said, "Mr Homer?"

"She's gone then, Darren. Wales. Where we planned to go, I suppose? Ffestiniog?"

"Yes," I said.

"Ask him about Dad!" Sally said fiercely in my ear. "Quick!"

"Mr Homer," I asked. "Do you know where Dad is?"

"We split up this afternoon," he said. "They were retreating. They dumped us off." A sort of sob in his voice. "Like sacks of potatoes. We were in their way. He said he was heading back for you, to pick you up."

"Where are you, Mr Homer?"

"Melton Mowbray." He sounded impatient now.

"Where's that?" I asked. "I've never heard of it."

"Near Leicester. Look, Darren. I have to go. I shouldn't be here anyway. I broke in. If my wife comes back, but I don't expect she will, let her know I've headed for Ffestiniog too. You'll do that for me, won't you?"

"Yes."

He put the phone down.

"Dad's safe! He's coming back!" I shouted to Sally. I forgave him on the spot for having made us wait. I forgave Sally for having made me wait.

4

The traffic slackened off as the evening wore on. I began to listen to it with a kind of eagerness instead of trying to blot it out. It wasn't just taking people away. A vehicle somewhere was bringing Dad home. It became a friendlier, more reassuring sound. I listened for a car drawing up outside our house or braking to a halt on the bottom road. I began to have happier thoughts. The meeting with Budge had brought memories back of my first year at the new school. I'd been lost and life was an intense burden. Dad had known it. He'd done everything possible to help me. He'd been great then, which must have been an effort for he was still recovering from the loss of his job. Then later, when I'd begun to accept school and settle down with new friends, Budge had begun to plague me. We went to different schools – he to the same one as Alex – but he seemed to pop up everywhere. He latched on to my fatness, my shyness, Dad's predicament. I quite seriously thought of killing myself. Then one night, tall and strong and grim, Dad had come striding through the dust of the latest beating and shaken Budge like a rat till he'd blubbered like a four-year-old, begged for mercy and wet himself in front of a jeering circle of children.

In the night there came another noise, the drone of planes overhead. Which way were they going? East or west? Were they ours or the Red Army's? More than once I drew back the curtains and tried to see them, but I saw nothing.

A wind blew up, tossing and turning branches of the trees, and rattling doors and windows. In the end a kind of terror replaced my hopeful feeling. I lay awake in the darkness listening to these noises, imagining ghosts, monsters, burglars, every frightening thing. I put the radio on once, low so as not to wake Sally, and heard "the army was standing up to the opposition" and "consolidating its position". Suddenly I couldn't have cared less about our army. The army had taken Dad away. Where was he? Surely he should have been back by now?

Once I woke, in the early hours – woken it seemed in a dream by knocking at the front door. When I sat up in bed, however, all I could hear was the sound of branches sawing against each other. I turned over and went back into a doze.

Sunlight woke me. Somehow I'd fallen into a deep sleep and overslept into the bargain. I rubbed my eyes and rolled out of bed. It was really late, ten o'clock. From the window I saw it was another sunny day, but windier, with white clouds chasing across the sky. Sally was up before me. I called her as I went downstairs. Dad must have arrived in the night. They'd let me sleep on. I slid down the bannister.

Dad wasn't there and the back door was ajar. I called Sally from the doorway. The wind carried my voice away. What would Dad say if he came back and found her gone? I began to run across the lawn then turned back to lock the door behind me before then jumping over the hedge and running down the slope towards the stream. As I ran I glanced at the road. The traffic was more like a normal day's, only the odd car, moving fast. I jumped the stream and got to the hide-out. I called up. No answer. She wasn't there. I panicked.

I jumped out of the tree, jarring every bone in my body,

and ran back up the bank. Half-way up Sally darted down at me.

"Where have you been?" I demanded angrily.

"Sshh!" she went.

"What?"

She clapped her hand roughly over my mouth. "Shut up!" she urged me. "Someone's broken in next door."

"What?" I said, still too loud. Suddenly I grasped it. "Who?"

"A car stopped down on the road. A big blue one. I saw the man from my hide-out and followed him. He sneaked along below the hedge and saw the window we broke yesterday. He climbed in."

"How long ago?"

"About ten minutes."

We were whispering now, crouched below the Homers' hedge.

"It's lucky he didn't spot our door. You left it open," I said to her.

"It was luckier still he didn't hear you calling," Sally said with a flash of spirit. "What are you going to do? Call the police?"

"The police?" It occurred to me I hadn't seen a policeman for ages. "What kind of man is he?"

"I don't know," she said. "I thought it might be Mr Homer, till he turned round – or even Dad. Shouldn't we do something about him? He's stealing."

I stood up and gazed at the back of the Homers'. I didn't feel at all brave about 'having to do something'. Do what? Tackle him? How? Then the man suddenly appeared at the window. I threw myself down on the ground.

"He's carrying things," I hissed.

We heard him clamber out of the window, then come running across the lawn. I grabbed Sally's hand, pulled her up and made her run away with me along the bank. I imagined this monster thudding after us, but when I took a quick look he was running down towards the road. He dropped one of the bags he'd been carrying, but didn't turn round to pick it up. A couple of minutes later we heard a car roar off on the road below. We went to investigate the bag. It was full of tins of food.

That was the beginning of a very bad day for us.

Later I made Sally come with me up into the estate. She wanted to wait for Dad, but I left him a note on the kitchen table and insisted she came. We went straight up Keats Avenue to the shops, seeing no one on the way, not even the old people I'd seen last time staring out from behind the nets. When we got to the shops I had a terrible shock. All of them were boarded up.

I stood and stared around. Then it dawned on me.

Sally suddenly began to cry. "They've left us behind," she sobbed.

"What do you mean?" I knew exactly what she meant. I just didn't want to hear her saying it.

"Don't be stupid!" Sally stamped her foot. "How many people have you seen this morning except that thief? They've all gone. We're the only ones left. Just us."

The estate was dead.

I turned on Sally. "This is all your fault!" I shouted.

I remembered the knocking I'd heard in my 'dream'. It hadn't just been a dream. We'd missed being evacuated.

The traffic had stopped on the bottom road. Nothing, not a thing, moved. I missed the noise of what I'd hated before. There was an eerie silence in which the only sounds were the wind in the branches, and now and then a bird calling out. There weren't even any cats or dogs – at least not near our road.

Dad had had a long time to come home. Perhaps the vehicle in which he was travelling had run out of petrol. Perhaps. It was an effort to kid myself into thinking everything was all right.

In the afternoon a plane flew over, low, below the white clouds, without markings. Another plane came rushing after it. I thought I heard a distant explosion moments after. It might have been my imagination.

At about four a car came charging along the bottom road. We ran out of the house, but it had skidded round the corner and away before we'd even had a chance to see it. The driver was going like a mad thing, as if the devil was after him.

The radio said nothing except a brief announcement that "our troops are withstanding the enemy", which is what they'd said in the night. Every now and then the station gave off a terrible crackling sound which drowned out the words.

"The radio's had it," Sally pronounced. "Trust it to go now."

"I think the station's being jammed," I said. This was a guess. "They can do that to enemy radio stations. Blot them out."

"Will the Red Army come here?" Sally asked.

"I'm not sure," I said. But it was true the next vehicles to travel along the bottom road might be the Red Army's – I somehow didn't trust the broadcast about our army standing up to them. And could there be any more vehicles on our side left to come? "With all these empty houses we'll have plenty of places to hide," I said.

"When's Dad coming?" Sally asked peevishly. "I want to go to Wales. We'll be safe there."

"He'll come," I said.

"Perhaps he's already gone there like Mr and Mrs Homer. Perhaps he thinks we've gone with everyone else. Perhaps he's looking for us there in one of those camps he talked about. We made a mistake."

"No!" I said. "He wouldn't have. Remember – Mr Homer said on the phone he was coming here."

"But he might," Sally said sulkily. "You know he might. We shouldn't have stayed."

I lost my temper.

"He wouldn't have done a thing like that!" I shouted. "You're stupid! You're a girl! You're not old enough!"

Sally was quiet a moment, then she said, "I wouldn't blame him," very quietly.

I hit her hard across the cheek. I hit her so hard her head rocked to one side.

I was so worked up I couldn't even apologise for doing such a terrible thing. I went into the front room and listened to the radio playing music then crackling whenever an announcer began to speak. After a time the station went off the air altogether. I fiddled with the tuning knob but all the stations that were broadcasting were in foreign languages except Radio British People's Homeland which was broadcasting non-stop pop and ignoring the war altogether.

There was no electricity and by the evening the cold water taps didn't work either. The hot taps were okay for cold water, though I didn't know why. Sally and I sat in the kitchen. Neither of us said so but we were both listening for Dad's footsteps outside. It was the second night like this. We didn't speak about my hitting her either. We opened two of the tins of food the man had abandoned in the morning. It made it less like stealing that he'd taken them first. All our own tins had been eaten. The food in the fridge had gone off. If you opened the door there was a revolting smell. We'd had no milk for two days. Our hands and faces were dirty. We'd washed, but the soap and cold water from the hot tap didn't seem to get rid of the grime. We were running out of clean clothes.

As we sat in the gathering darkness, both at the end of our tether, absolutely sick of one another, I decided that tomorrow we must attempt to follow everyone else away from here even if Dad had told us to stay put. We would walk if necessary.

When Sally had gone upstairs to sleep I fiddled with the radio again. There were only crackles from the BBC but a station called Voice of the Red Army was broadcasting loud and clear on a nearby frequency.

"We have achieved our objectives," the announcer said. "We have captured all the ex-American missile sites. However, during the action, in contravention of all agreements, British forces launched nuclear weapons. At 14.30 hours this afternoon our soldiers were forced to make a limited retaliation. I repeat: our forces were obliged to retaliate."

He didn't say what this special retaliation had been. I didn't think much about it at the time. What naivety – I'd not seen an explosion. It didn't concern me.

If only we had started running, walking, crawling – anything to get away.

5

The weather had changed completely next morning. Grey clouds raced across the sky. It had rained heavily, the ground was sodden and every five minutes another squall swept over the estate. Setting off to walk to Wales was clearly out of the question. I crept downstairs and fiddled with the radio, but I found I'd left it on all night.

I put a note on the kitchen table telling Sally not to leave the house. I had an idea. It meant stealing, but surely our desperate situation excused that? Surely the threats of summary execution for looting wouldn't apply to us? If I could find a car with petrol I felt confident I could drive it safely since there was no other traffic on the road. We could travel to Wales on four wheels. Walk? What an idiot I had been! Things had changed. I was king around here till further notice! I could do more or less as I wanted!

The rain came down hard as I went up Keats Avenue. I began a methodical search, trying every garage door, going round the backs of houses if there was a drive. The first couple of dozen houses yielded nothing. Then, going round the back of the next house, I came across a nasty sight – a dead dog curled up in a corner against a wall. I began to notice other dead animals – dogs and cats, rats (where had they come from?), a rabbit dead in its hutch, bodies of birds, a fox. Why all this death? It was summer. Surely all these creatures wouldn't have died of hunger, not even the abandoned dogs?

I forgot them completely though when I found the side door of a garage unlocked and an old Cortina inside. I rushed to open the garage door. Next I set about getting the car started. I'd seen car thieves do it often enough on film, but luckily a key caught my eye, taped on the far side of the beam across the garage roof. It opened the car and turned the ignition on. The fuel gauge read three-quarters full. I was in luck.

My first effort at driving was a disaster. I started the engine and the car took two jumps backwards into a work bench. I stood on the clutch and manhandled the gear lever into neutral. Then I repositioned the seat. This jammed me up against the steering wheel but my feet reached the pedals. I started the car again and with a horrendous scraping noise got it into first. I revved and eased up the clutch. The car leaped once more. At least it was forwards this time but there was a burning smell which had me scrambling out until I remembered the handbrake. After this I began to do better. I eased out of the garage and down the short drive. I turned the steering wheel too early passing into the road, which crunched the near-side, but I didn't get out to inspect the damage. I was moving, wasn't I? I pointed the car downhill. In a moment I was changing into second, then third. In fact I got a little too confident. I braked so spectacularly outside our house, I was nearly impaled on the steering column.

Sally was in the kitchen. I wanted to boast about my driving ability. One look at her made me forget all that. She looked awful, her face a sickly yellow colour. She was shivering violently, but when I put my hand to her forehead I could feel she was feverish.

"I was sick," she said. "I managed to get to the toilet."

There was a stench on her breath. "I ache all over, Darren. What is it?"

I had no idea what to do. I'd never seen anyone look so ill. I went to the cupboard where we kept our tin of medicines and bandages. The only thing that seemed the faintest use was the aspirins. I gave her three. She had a job swallowing them and was sick again immediately. I washed her face and hands – it had to be in cold water – then carried her on to the settee in the other room. "I'm cold," she said, hunching herself up. In a short time she became delirious. I tried to make her talk sensibly – I tried desperately hard – but it was no use. Then I remembered that the phone had been working yesterday.

From Mrs Homer's I dialled 999. The phone rang out but no one answered. I dialled the number again and again. No one was answering.

Sally got worse by the minute. Her forehead was boiling. She was muttering under her breath, then crying out loud. Most of it was nonsense, but some made me want to cry, about Dad and Mum. Some of it was about me. This wasn't anything to do with having hit her yesterday, was it? I hadn't caused this? (Even today, years on, this doubt lingers.)

I could only think of one thing to do: carry out my original plan and drive to Wales. I took the road atlas and all the blankets I could find to the car. Then I carried out Sally, laid her carefully on the back seat and covered her up. She was heavy and made my arms ache. I ran back and locked up the house. I left a scribbled note for Dad on the kitchen table.

The rain had become continuous. I found the switch for the windscreen wipers. Then, when I started the car, I found it was facing in the wrong direction. I would have to back out of the road. I struggled with the gear lever, got it into every gear but reverse, and stalled it a dozen times before I managed to move. Sally was like a rag doll with sweat pouring off her in little rivers. I didn't feel too good myself either. My reversing was awful. I hit the pavement countless times (the car seemed attracted to it) and mounted it twice, but eventually we were out of the cul-de-sac.

It was really pouring down as I turned out on to the bottom road at the spot where I'd last seen Mrs Homer. If only we'd gone with her. Someone could be looking after Sally now. How far did I have to drive before I'd find a doctor? I put my foot down and pushed the car up to over forty. I was still in third and it shook like an old tin can: which was what it really was, a Cortina built ten years before the Blitz. I skidded on a flooded corner. Just in time, some instinct told me to take my foot off the accelerator and let the car right itself. I sat and trembled for a minute before forcing myself to drive on.

There were other hazards. Every now and then there was an abandoned car. These were mostly on the left-hand side so I began to drive on the right. However, just round a sharp corner a car had been parked on the right. I pulled on the wheel so sharply (I had the impression it was coming towards me) that we swung right round. Our boot crunched into the stationary vehicle and I was facing the wrong way. I decided the most sensible thing to avoid complicated manoeuvring would be to head up a side street, then turn back into the road I wanted. It might have been sensible, but it wasn't simple. I got lost in a maze of deserted back streets. It was ten minutes before I reached the abandoned car again.

In the back seat Sally's temperature seemed more normal and she'd fallen into a deep sleep. I made myself drive less frantically.

The next difficulty I ran into was in a place where the road split without saying clearly which way Wolverhampton was (the quickest road into Wales I'd worked out). Unluckily I chose left. The road took a sharp bend then passed under a railway bridge. The bridge was low and the road narrow. A double-decker in the blue-and-white livery of West Midlands buses had got stuck under it. The impact had torn off half the bus's roof. There was a gap between the bus and the side of the bridge I might have edged through, but I wasn't confident enough to try.

I began the laborious business of backing to the fork. I must have improved because I don't remember hitting anything except the kerb once or twice. I took the right-hand turning and drove on. At the top of a steepish hill I came to some traffic lights which weren't working. I turned left, down a street of shops.

This street, however, wasn't completely deserted. A dozen dogs were roaming it. Most of them drew back on to the pavement at the sound of the car, but as I passed some came out into the road. They started chasing after me, not aggressively but as if they wanted human company. There was glass all over the road where many of the shop windows were smashed in. Were there people here? I kept a wary eye open. I'd seen TV documentaries of people in America and other countries during the Blitz looting.

I saw another disturbing thing before I reached the bottom of the street. My eye was on the mirror when one of the dogs racing after us keeled over – just like that – dead. I had a vivid recollection of the corpses on the estate. They had been inexplicable too.

By now the rain had stopped. A weak sun filtered through the clouds and cheered up the streets. The road surface quickly began to dry. I took more notice of what I was passing. It was inconceivable that everyone had gone. Though I saw no one I saw signs of people: corner shops broken into – smashed windows – and many more dead animals and birds, even a sheep lying in the road. What had they all died of?

That Russian broadcast last night. The animals – Sally's condition – were they connected? I slowed down and glanced round at Sally and felt her forehead. She was boiling hot again. What had that broadcast said about retaliation? Had I missed something else! The retaliation – what had it been?

There was a halt sign where my road joined a dual

carriageway. A notice said *Drive Carefully In This Borough.*
Thank You. I stopped the car and opened the road atlas. As
I did so a car whizzed past me along the dual carriageway.
It was bursting at the seams with people. I pulled out and
put my foot down too. I flashed my lights and hooted but
it just drew away. On a water-logged corner I went into another
skid. I lowered my speed. The other car had gone. It was
a job to know whether to be cheered up or depressed by my
fleeting glimpse of other human beings. The town appeared
ahead on a very steep hill with what looked like the ruins of
a castle on its top. Half-way up I had to turn right at some
traffic-lights that seemed to be set permanently at red.

Two corners later I caught up with the car that had passed
us. It was a blazing wreck piled up on the pavement against
the wall of a Co-op. I rushed past and stopped. There was
no hope of anyone being alive among such terrible flames but
I opened my door. Even at a distance I could feel the heat.
Then it struck me the wreck was so total this couldn't have
been an accident. The car looked as if it had been bombed
or mined. Perhaps I was travelling just in front of the Red
Army. Perhaps our army assumed that everyone English had
already got out. I slammed the car door and drove on,
suddenly fearful for my own life. I drove with utter
recklessness, skidding and squealing round corners – just as
the other car had done, as if it had been racing against time.
If I drove over a mine, death would be instantaneous, wouldn't
it? Or could you outpace the blast from one?

Suddenly in front of me I could see the motorway running
across the landscape on a tall embankment. I put my foot
down, and down and down. The car went faster and faster.
The motorway seemed to represent some kind of frontier.
Beyond it I would be safe.

But that wasn't to be. In the mirror I saw a fat shadow
tearing up the road behind me. At the same time, a line of
explosions tore up the tarmac ahead of me.

I braked. My chest buckled against the steering column.

Behind me there was a thud. Sally had been jolted off the seat on to the car floor.

A helicopter landed in front of us and two men jumped straight out. They were wearing something strange on their heads. I didn't have time to see what because one of them fired into the air above the car. I ducked, hitting my head on the wheel. The Red Army, I thought. All the horror stories came back, the accounts of lingering cruel deaths. Idiotically I remembered a propaganda item that said how marvellously kind they were to children. Did I qualify as a child?

One of them wrenched open the driver's door, grabbed me with both hands and dragged me out.

"Where've you come from? Answer me!"

A plastic hand pulled me upright from the road.

"Where've you come from? Where do you think you're going?"

I could tell he meant to hit me. I tried to double up to take the blow. Oh God, they were going to kill me or shoot me for being a spy. But they were English. My body absorbed the blow. Then it hurt.

The other man spoke. "Not so heavy. It's only a kid."

"So?"

"There's another on the floor in the back. A girl."

"Get her out."

I heard the back door being opened – then quickly slammed shut.

"She has it! What did I tell you?"

The man who had his hand on me jerked me upright so I was looking into his face. Except it wasn't a face. He was wearing a protective mask through which you could only see his eyes. I began to suspect.

"Where are you from?"

I stammered out my address.

"Deliberately trying to spread it," the man who was holding me said. He was going to hit me again. He did. It was relief almost, the red-hot pain in my stomach, to get it over with.

I felt damaged inside. "Infecting others." My ears buzzed as if he'd hit me there. I didn't know what he was talking about. I didn't know what I'd done wrong. I had no clue. I tried to tell him so.

"My sister needs a doctor."

"Why weren't you evacuated?" the second man asked. He had a softer voice and manner behind his mask.

"We waited for Dad. He didn't come. The council people must have missed us. Everyone else had gone when we went to look."

"Fat fool," the first man said.

"Your sister – what's wrong with her?" the more sympathetic one asked. "Exactly."

I gasped out her symptoms.

"I told you. They've got it," the man holding me said. "They're trying to give it us. Worse than the Reds."

"Got what?" I shouted in frustration, not caring whether he hit me again or not. These men were British soldiers. They ought to have been on my side. They ought to have been helping me with Sally. They ought to have lifted her into their helicopter and flown her to the nearest hospital. They ought to have been friendly.

"Are you stupid? The germ bomb the Red Army dropped on the East Midlands, near Leicester! It's been raining. The wind carried it this way. You've all got it. Your sister, you, everyone who didn't get away in time. All of you. It's raining poison this very moment."

The retaliation. Leicester – wasn't that where Dad had been?

"Fatal," one of them was saying. "Even the Reds have been broadcasting warnings. They've scared themselves."

They began discussing me as if I wasn't there.

"Shoot them," I heard. "Kindest way ..." "... haven't got the heart ..." "... turn them back and make sure they go ..." "... give them a chance ..."

I was pushed back into the car.

"Listen," the more kindly one said. The other was swearing. "Go back the way you came. Go back home. You might survive. If you don't go we shoot you. It's as simple as that. That's our orders. Some fools didn't stop just now. Now hurry! Turn the car round and don't come back this way again. Stay where you came from."

"But I can't look after her. What if the Russians come?"

"They won't. They know what this bomb can do better than us. They dropped it."

"Never come back," the other man said. He slammed the door on me. "Forget England."

"He'll have it too," he said as I started the engine. "Really it would have been kinder ... " I didn't hear the rest.

I swung the car round, mounting the verge. The soldiers stood watching me, their guns trained after the car.

Sally had some terrible disease. That had finally registered. I probably had it too. I felt more or less lousy anyway. I would die if I had it. The disease was so terrible they were stopping anyone joining the evacuees. They were writing us off. Forget England.

I slowed down, trying to remember my way back. The shadow of the helicopter came into my mirror again. I took a turning right in sheer panic. The shadow came up close behind us. I could hear the noise of the helicopter. I thought: They've changed their minds. They're going to kill us after all. I swung the car up another road and found we were in the street where the car had crashed. The blaze had died down. It was smouldering now. There was a sweet smell which I imagined was charred flesh. I felt sick. I suppose those people had known they wouldn't be let through unless they outran the helicopter. I turned down the hill towards the dual carriageway. The helicopter shadow left us. It whirled away over some waste ground towards factories in the distance, searching for other refugees.

A mile further on I stopped to see to Sally. I'd not even

looked at her since my emergency stop had thrown her on to the car floor. She was so still that for a moment I thought she was dead, but she suddenly said, "Darren. Where are we?" From where I was sitting I couldn't move her so I pulled the handbrake on even harder, got out and manhandled her back onto the seat.

"Sally. Can you hear me?"

She was gone again, without answering.

I tried to think clearly. Was there any point in going home? No one was there. But if I didn't, where else could I take Sally? There were no hospitals or nurses or doctors left. Or firemen or policemen. No one to help. Then I remembered that street of looted shops. What was there to stop me from breaking into a chemist's to get medicine for her? The only problem was, I didn't know what she'd got, and the soldiers had spoken as if she were incurable.

The sun had been shining for some time. It had turned into a cheerful afternoon, but suddenly I began to cry. I cried for Sally, and for Dad who must be dead if he'd still been near Leicester when this terrible bomb was dropped – Mr Homer too. Then my tears dried up. I just felt rage against everyone who'd escaped what Sally had, against the two soldiers in their stupid masks, against Mrs Homer and anyone else who'd got away, against the Russians. Especially I felt rage against Dad who'd let himself be dragged off. If he'd been shot resisting, *like a man*, at least Sally would have been evacuated.

I drove on quickly, glaring, barely conscious of the road. Ten minutes later I found myself at the crossroads at the bottom of the street of shops. I pulled myself together. I'd give the chemists a try. Eventually I found two chemists near a phone box. I stopped the car and got out.

The quiet in the street was a midnight silence; I could hear my own breathing. Then I heard a rattle which must have been the wind stirring something in one of the looted shops. I froze and my heart pounded. Eventually I got the courage together to leave the car and cross the road. My shoes crunched glass. Ominously not one dog appeared, Had they all died – suddenly, just like that?

I stared inside first one chemist's and then the other. I was scared of their shadowy interiors. Then I saw torches on display inside one of the windows. I stepped inside the broken glass and grabbed the largest. There were batteries in blister packs. I took a pack of what looked the right size and retreated outside to fix the torch.

What the torchlight showed gave me no cause for hope. The shelves of medicine held cough sweets, cough mixtures, lozenges, hayfever pills, iron tablets, but nothing suitable for Sally. I looked through them twice then, in sheer frustration, swept the whole lot on to the floor. Bottles smashed, pills and sweets rolled everywhere. I stamped on them. There was a sweet, sickly smell of oozing medicaments.

My shoes stuck to the floor as I flashed the torch around the shelves behind the counter. There was a closed cupboard as wide as the span of my arms from shoulder height to the roof. I remembered that only someone who was specially qualified was allowed to dispense doctors' prescriptions. This was where they kept the stuff that really did you good.

I clambered over the counter and rattled the cupboard doors – locked of course. There was a locked drawer under the counter and I couldn't open that either. The key to the cupboard was probably in it. I grabbed the only heavy object handy, a stool, and attacked the medicine cupboard door with that. I battered and battered. The door withstood every blow. In the end I just had to give up, sweat dripping off me and my arms aching. I had some energy left though. I went on a rampage of destruction through the shop, smashing everything I could reach. I don't know what came over me. Eventually I stopped from sheer exhaustion. It was then I spotted a large screwdriver my blows had knocked off a shelf. It must have been kept behind some goods. In a moment I had wrenched the cupboard door open.

Hundreds and hundreds of bottles and tins and boxes stared at me. My heart sank. Where to start? I hadn't the faintest idea what I was searching for. I got up on a stool and began to play the torch along row after row of medicines. Most of them had meaningless trade names, nothing to tell you what they were for. I took things down, one after the other, seeking enlightenment. Then I came across a large bottle of small white tablets, marked 'Penicillin.' I seized it. Liquid penicillin had to be kept in a fridge, I remembered. I used to take it for the bad colds I got when I was younger. It was used for worse illnesses too. We'd learnt about its discovery in lessons once. I jumped down off the stool.

I hesitated before I stepped out through the broken window. Perhaps there were others who'd got left behind. I hadn't thought of that before. They might have heard me. I also felt ashamed of the needless destruction I'd caused. I was as scared to leave the shop as I had been to go into it.

Sally's forehead was now really boiling, hotter than it had ever been before. I started the car up and drove like a maniac towards home. I screeched into the estate and overshot the end of the cul-de-sac. I parked on some waste ground.

I wasn't sure whether Sally was still alive as I carried her back into the house. Her chest hardly moved as I laid her on the settee. I tried to feel her pulse but I couldn't find it. When I laid my ear on her chest I could just hear her heart beating very, very faintly, far away.

I threw every blanket and coat I could find over her. Then I prised open her mouth, put a tablet of penicillin on her tongue and tried to get her to swallow it with a drop of water. She gulped for air and spat the tablet back at me. Holding her up, lying her down, the effect was the same – the tablet came back.

She seemed hot enough to explode. The tablets were no use if she couldn't keep them down. I got a clean tea towel, soaked it in cold water and wrapped it across her forehead. What else? Nothing. There was nothing else I could do. I sat a few minutes by her side, then went out into the garden. I felt angry again. I wanted to break things, as I had in the shop but much worse. I would have liked to have knocked down the street, the whole estate. Sally was dying.

The sun burnt my arms. The rain clouds had gone. The sky, the air, the plants, the ground – they must be full of whatever was killing Sally. I wanted to be like the poison, to destroy everything.

Sally died early that evening. An hour later I got a spade from the Homers' shed and dug a hole for her in one of our flower borders. I didn't mark the spot. It wasn't hard to remember – next to the fifth and sixth paving stones of the path. As I dug a thought went through my mind: I ought to dig a hole next to Sally's the right size for myself. Then when I felt ill enough I could just lie down in it and wait for the end. I was sure I'd get the disease if I hadn't got it already. I knew all about the killer diseases American, Russian and British scientists had been developing over the years. Dad had told me about them and how they'd used them in the war in Thailand. Hadn't I been feeling ill all day? Yet when I went back in the house and threw myself down on the settee I felt better. I rattled the radio, trying to get it to work, but it wouldn't make a sound.

When it started to get dark I couldn't stand being in the house. I put on a coat and went into the estate. I took a small axe with me. I didn't want anyone to come near me, if there was anyone else left.

I went up Keats Avenue, taking a good look at each house. The doors of the garage from which I'd stolen the car still stood wide open but three houses further up another house's front door was open. I stopped short. This morning it hadn't been like that.

I went to the house and saw the door glass had been

smashed to reach the lock. I stood on the threshold. "Anyone there?" I called, but no one answered. I went in. There was just about enough light to look into the rooms from the hall. Then I checked upstairs. The house had been turned upside down, cupboards pulled open, contents of drawers scattered over the floors. Most of the tinned food had gone from the kitchen.

Things became unbearable. Suddenly I became aware of the axe in my hands. I went into the house's front room and put the axe through the TV. I liked the sound. There was a hi-fi set Dad would have loved. I broke it up. I slashed into the speakers, pulled the records out on to the floor and smashed them. I cracked the mirror and poured bottles of drink over the settee before I ripped that up too. I hacked holes in the carpet and smashed two shelves of stupid fancy ornaments. Then I went through the house and systematically broke and ripped and smashed everything. It was very dark when I finished. I could hardly see what I was doing. I went back into the front room. There was a shelf of encyclopaedias and I dragged the books into the middle of the floor and ripped out the pages. There were fifteen of them and it must have taken me the best part of an hour to make a heap of them in the middle of the floor. My arms and hands ached when I'd finished as if I'd done a day's cement mixing.

I poured lighter fuel over the books, then lit a match. There was a photo fluttering about the floor. I looked hard at the photo by matchlight and remembered the couple, though I'd only known them to nod to. I used the photo to light the bonfire. Then I left the house.

6

The day after Sally died was very silent: no traffic, no voices, far fewer bird noises than usual.

I stayed in the house without once setting foot outside. I didn't even look out of the windows. There was a smell of burning. It crept into the house. Would I have really been able to smell it? Or was it conscience?

I was waiting for a sound, the sound of Dad's key in the door. There was no logic in it but I'd become convinced again that he was alive. I'd survived, so might he. Whoever had broken into the house on Keats Avenue yesterday had survived too. And Mr Homer had been alive the day *before* the germ bomb had been dropped. That was a thought. Dad might have been miles away from Leicester by then. He'd have had time to get to the safe area. Or perhaps he'd been in that car the helicopter had blown up.

While I waited I dozed or wandered round the rooms, poking into every corner as if I'd never lived there before or it wasn't my own home. I spent most time in Dad's bedroom or investigating a bureau in the front room which he had never actually told us to keep out of, but which Sally and I had never opened without permission.

I felt really guilty, but now it was my right to look.

He had been a real hoarder. There were bills for electricity, rent, rates, going back years, all in the right order, filed in large envelopes. There was a box file of guarantees for anything we'd ever bought, and some things I didn't remember, brochures for holiday resorts we'd visited, clipped together with postcards bought when we'd been there, photographs by the hundred, letters Mum must have written to him before they were married, even his twenty-first birthday cards. Eventually I put everything except the photos in a cardboard box. Then I spent several hours looking at the photos – photos of Mum, of Dad, of Sally and me, photos of relatives and places, photos of people I didn't recognise or have names for. Mum was a person I didn't remember well. She'd died long ago, just after Sally's birth. There were also a lot of photos of me with Alex, me looking podgy as usual, Alex looking grown-up beside me. Dad had been fond of Alex. It somehow showed in the pictures. It came into my mind that perhaps he'd have preferred Alex for a son instead of me.

In the end I threw all the photos except those which were of Dad into the box together with an envelope of clippings from newspapers about the accident in which Mum had died, her funeral notice in the paper, her death certificate. I spread Dad's photos out over the floor and studied them minutely. Then I went into the kitchen and waited.

I tried to think of everyone but him. I was dreading confronting him when he came. I was petrified. There was so much to blame him for. What had happened to me was all his fault. But I'd loved and admired him so much – questioned him perhaps over the last year, but still admired him beyond reason. And loved him. No question of that.

All that had changed. Now I hated him. I kept telling myself that while trying to prevent myself from thinking of him.

When he hadn't come by nine I knew that dead or alive he wasn't coming. I threw his photos into the box too, took the box outside and burned it. I pinned a notice on the back door saying "Sally died. It was your fault. Don't come in here." I didn't consciously listen for his footsteps or his knock after that.

Next day I woke up lonely but clean – not physically clean: I probably stank, but clean of family, of every tie. I had slept downstairs in the front. I tidied that room, then the whole house. Now my Robinson Crusoe existence began. I made preparations, organised, made lists, inventories, plans.

By midday all that was over. I sank to a low point of suicidal despair. I didn't mourn Sally and my father. I mourned myself, my wasted life.

Alex had been at the back of my mind all this time. Seeing the photos of us together had rekindled my memory of him. Perhaps he'd got left behind. Perhaps like me he'd survived.

In the afternoon my obsession with him took over. I drove the mile or so to his house.

As soon as I got out of the car I realised the futility of having come. Why should there be anyone else? I peered through Alex's windows. He certainly wasn't at home. After a few minutes I got back in the car and drove home.

But about midnight I was woken with a start by some noise that shouldn't have been there. People were in the road.

I raised myself on an elbow to look through the black square of the window.

The footsteps stopped. There were low voices, a car door opened. I thought: people have come to the house. Dad! It was him. I found I wanted him, on whatever terms.

Then I realised it was the door of my car which I'd left right outside the house.

A moment later the intruders crept towards my window. I rolled off the settee and lay out of sight. A second later a torch shone in the room and played round it.

"Odd," a voice whispered, "it being abandoned like that with the key in. Is someone about?"

Whose voice was that? It was familiar.

"Here? No. They would have gone." The second voice was Alex's. I relaxed, but not for long.

"Who? Who do you know living down here?"

"You know."

"Who?"

Budge was cruelly insistent.

"Darren of course."

"Fatso?"

"Yes. Him."

Did Alex admit it reluctantly?

"Come on, Budge," Alex said impatiently. "I'm sick of hanging round. Let's get back. I didn't come down here on purpose. I'd forgotten about him completely."

"Darren – that little git. So this is his place."

Alex had moved away. "The others will be waiting. You told them not to eat till we got back."

"So what? They can do what they're told. A pity I didn't do something about him the other day when I had the chance. Boy, wouldn't he frizzle! Have you any matches?"

"No. And if you have to burn them, set fire to places *after* you've seen what's inside. Come on. I'm hungry. You weren't up all last night on watch."

"Listen, Alex," Budge said. "Just listen – "

"What?" Alex was walking back across the lawn. He sounded browned off. "What, Budge?"

I heard Budge hurry after him.

A couple of minutes later my car reversed out of the cul-de-sac.

7

Next morning I went to the shops in the estate. I desperately needed to find batteries for my radio. It was idiotic not to know what was really happening. All I actually knew was what two trigger-happy plastic suited soldiers had screamed at me.

And I needed, even more urgently in the short term, I *had* to know where Budge was based. The nearer that was, the more urgent it was for me to get away. For he would be back in the cul-de-sac one day and that day I might not hear him coming. Alex too. It hurt, but as long as he and Budge were together Alex counted as my enemy.

It was a bright sunny morning. Looking out across the park I had the illusion for a second that I was setting out on a Sunday morning walk before the heat of the day.

I went up Keats Avenue, in darts and rushes, then staying still and gazing at every house window, up every path and drive, from every angle, behind each hedge and wall, analysing every sound.

However I hurried past the house I'd set on fire. Its downstairs was completely gutted. If I was capable of that, what were others capable of? Frizzle, hadn't Budge said?

What if the fire had spread? The whole estate could have

been engulfed. What if Budge had been carrying matches last night? His violence in and out of school had been legendary, and that with the near certainty of being caught and punished. And what about Alex? If I'd gathered anything last night it was that he was Budge's second-in-command. How much had he changed? And had he been perfect then, when we'd been best friends? Hadn't it been a possessive sort of friendship, with him apt to take his moods out on me and stop me making friends with others?

At last I reached the crossroads. What would have been a five minute walk had taken me over half an hour. I was sweating heavily and quite past recognising anything suspicious. I crouched behind the last wall that gave any cover. Everything seemed the same at first glance, then I noticed something wrong. The shops were still boarded up, but there was glass on the pavement. The reason was simple. The boards had been taken off, the windows broken, then the boards replaced to make it look as if nothing had happened. Budge and Alex and their gang at work?

I ran low and direct to the newsagent's. My back prickled as I put down my rucksack and used the axe blade to lever off the boards across the door. I saw at once that my guess was right. All the glass in the door had gone.

I squeezed inside, switched on my torch and moved across the shop. Someone had knocked over the battery stand, but I found several blister packs of the size I wanted on the floor, plus some replacements for the torch. I stuffed them in the rucksack and played my torch around the rest of the shop. I told myself not to be greedy, not to stay any longer than necessary. Cigarettes were no good to me, but I took matches. I also picked up a few comics and a couple of car magazines. Then I raided the sweet and chocolate counter. Someone had been there before me, but there was still plenty to weigh my bag down. I swept the torch round a last time. I had to go. I'd pressed my luck far enough. I turned towards the door.

My heart jumped. Someone was clambering in.

I backed off towards the counter and ducked down.

"This is ours. We're giving you ten seconds to get out." It was a man's voice, rough and low. I kept my head down and tightened my grip on the axe. There was a metallic click. "I'll kill you. Don't think I won't. Stand up."

I stood up. "Let me out," I said. "I don't mean to make trouble."

"You're not taking a thing," he said. "Not one item. These shops are ours."

"Whose are?" I asked in surprise. "You're not the newsagent, are you?" It was a real question for I wasn't quite sure.

"Ours," he said. "Go elsewhere. You'll take nothing from us. Steal elsewhere."

"Steal!" I said sharply. "That's a good one!"

"You've heard!" the man said. He stepped closer and suddenly snapped a powerful light in my face. "I know you," he said accusingly. "You're from further down. You've no right up here. Get your stuff from Netherend."

"That's miles away!" I protested. I turned away from the light. "I only came for batteries for my radio," I said as unprovocatively as I could. "I'll give you the rest back if you're that mean." I laid down my axe within easy reach but so he'd see it and started pulling the sweets and magazines back out of the rucksack. The torch followed what I was doing. He didn't say anything about the batteries. When all that was left was some blister packs and a token bag of sweets I slung the rucksack on my back and picked up my axe.

"You run all the estate?"

(I was getting the idea about gangs very quickly.)

"Around here," he said. "We stay up here. In our territory. I know your road. It's that cul-de-sac. Stay there."

"What about others?"

He didn't answer.

There were two lads of my own age skulking in a garden

59

across the street, cradling something in their arms. Guns? I was too naive to decide. All the same I took no chances.

I played the radio low.

"This is Her Majesty's Government broadcasting from Cardiff," said the first station I found. "No further contact has been reported between British and Enemy forces. An uneasy peace reigns. The Army and RAF continue to patrol the M5 and M6 motorways to prevent anyone left behind in the evacuation from crossing over into uncontaminated territory. It is believed that a very small number of people have survived the ravages of the disease which has also badly affected animal life. However scientists have established that survivors are also carriers of the disease and likely to remain permanent ones. The question of aid to these people will be considered within the next few days. Meanwhile any movement east, back into the affected areas is strictly forbidden. Offenders will be shot. Scientists consider the disease is likely to remain active for a considerable time. A precise definition of the affected area will be attempted as soon as possible.

"Other news. The Council for Scotland and the North will administer from Edinburgh and Newcastle. Discussions with the Red Army will be initiated when – "

I searched for another station. The next was broadcasting from London.

" – appeals to the population to remain calm. Conditions will return to normal as soon as practicable. The cowardly action of the British forces in launching nuclear tipped missiles on course for Moscow has been condemned throughout Europe and the rest of the world. If the Red Army had not succeeded in forcing the missiles down over an already devastated area in Germany it is apparent the consequences would have been catastrophic.

"Red Army forces are patrolling the eastern and southern areas affected by our retaliatory action. The civilian population is reminded that it is an offence punishable by immediate death to attempt to pass either in or out of the area."

In the afternoon Budge still lay heavy on my thoughts, that jolly face and twisted mind. The man in the shop didn't worry me a quarter as much even if he'd had me at the end of a gun. He'd been as frightened as me. I'd heard his voice quiver.

And Alex. Alex still drew me to him, Budge's right-hand man or not. I had it in mind that if I could get him on his own he could be persuaded to pal up with me again. Before that, though, he had to leave Budge.

But first I had to know where they were. I went away from the estate, down through the park, on to the road where all the traffic had been and past the factory which stood on the other side of the bridge, its great iron gates locked and chained.

I had with me a pair of binoculars I'd found in the Homers. Mr Homer had been a keen bird-spotter.

The road ran alongside the park, then bore right, uphill, away from it. Too soon I came across my first sign of Budge. On the right a road led off up a steep bank, back into a residential area. On a wall that held up the end of a garden was sprayed a message:

BUDGE RULES THE WORLD
DEATH TO INTRUDERS!

Someone had added in smaller joined-up letters:

okay?

I hurried past, dismayed to have found Budge practically on my doorstep.

The road levelled out. On the left was an old people's home, a modern two-storey building. I inspected every window, wondering whether it was possible someone had got left behind here, but I supposed it was the kind of place where a line of coaches would roll up and an official with a check-list made sure everyone was accounted for, not like our estate. There would probably be food supplies in the kitchen. I didn't need that man and his shops.

On the right-hand side of the road ran another stream. Beyond it was a steep grassy slope with two blocks of flats at the top. I crouched by a tree and stared at the windows for any sign of life. Past the flats I could see the roofs of houses. They were on Budge's road.

I moved on to a T-junction with another road and darted across to a grassy knoll on the far side. I looked back the way I'd come but even with binoculars I couldn't see as much as I wanted. I would have to go nearer.

I came back down off the knoll and crossed the road again. I followed the path up the bank and approached the doors of the second block. The lobby door was locked so I had to smash the glass and reach through to undo it. Inside it smelt foul beyond belief. I went up the stairs which were on the outer wall but on the side away from Budge's road. When I got to the top landing there was no way on to the roof except through a trap-door miles out of reach. So I used my axe again and smashed in the door of one of the flats that faced the right way. I found myself in a beautifully tidy lounge. Tidy - who cared? No one was coming back.

The glass doors on to the balcony were unbolted. I slid them slowly apart, then crouched looking over the parapet. I could see further than ever I'd have imagined. There was a ring of hills beyond the hills I was familiar with. Through a gap in them I could see flat ground. I focused my glasses and found I was staring at the motorway. At this distance it was all a bit of a blur but I could make out a helicopter and several large vehicles on the carriageways. Something was being built. I couldn't see what.

Closer to, however, I could see with astonishing clarity. I found the cul-de-sac with our house half-hidden by the tree on the opposite side of the road. I followed up Keats Avenue with the glasses and found the shops. There was no one near them, but when I began to systematically search the crossroad area I found that one of the side streets had been barricaded off at both ends. Something to do with the man at the shops this morning? It had to be.

I turned my attention nearer and brought my glasses to bear on Budge's adopted road. It was a pleasant-looking street. I quickly swept my glasses along it. There were sixty or seventy houses perhaps, all detached. Rich pickings to be had! I looked more carefully.

The street began and finished in steep rises. In the middle it was on the level and made a gentle S-shape. The first house I noticed having anything different about it was almost at the top of the rise, at my end. The ground floor windows of the house and the front door were boarded up. I looked more closely. One of the top floor windows was slightly ajar. Was someone living there? Was this Budge's headquarters? It wasn't the only boarded up house, but all the rest seemed totally sealed.

I watched this house and particularly this window for a quarter of an hour until a movement near the middle of the flat stretch of the road caught my eye. It was Alex! He and a couple of lads I didn't know were coming round from the back of another house, laden with boxes and bags. At the gate Alex rested his load and squinted up and down the street before beckoning the others forward. The procession made its way towards the far end of the road and turned into another house, Budge's HQ and warehouse, I supposed. As the crow flies it was not far from home, but by road it was a fair distance. That cheered me up a little.

I went back to searching the road, checking every minute or so on Budge's place, then the house which had the open window.

Half an hour later Alex and the other two returned carrying empty bags and boxes. They passed the house they'd come from originally and went in through the next gate. Alex tried the front door and windows, then led the others round the back. A moment later I heard the sound of glass breaking.

I watched till early evening. By then a further half a dozen houses had been broken into. It was food he was after, dried food, tinned food. He worked, and worked his little gang, as if his life depended on it. All this time Budge didn't appear once.

Just as I left I thought for a moment that I caught a glimpse of someone watching me from the part-open window of the boarded house. When I looked more closely with the binoculars, however, it was a shadow that didn't move.

8

They were working by floodlight at the motorway when I slipped into my observation post at the flats very early next morning. The sun began to rise. I watched it climb till the sky lost its sheen. I was numb with apprehension. I couldn't wait. I would confront Alex today. I would get it over with.

The first thing I noticed different in the road was 'my' Cortina. I spied it parked on the front drive of Budge's headquarters. After that there was little to do except watch and wait with what patience I could muster. The sun blazed down and the day became oppressively hot. The window of the barred-up house was still slightly ajar, but was it at a different angle? If someone was living there was it possible they hadn't been discovered by Budge? What would happen when Alex's looting parties reached there? Later in the morning I could have sworn I saw someone moving inside. After considerable reflection I decided I hadn't.

I'd brought my radio. As I flicked through the stations you'd have thought nothing extraordinary had happened. Radio 1 was playing pop, Radio 2 the old-fashioned stuff adults seemed to like, Radio 3 something screechy on violins, Radio 4 a news programme, "unavoidably delayed from last week", concerned with traffic congestion in New York. The Russian-run British Homeland station was just the same – old-fashioned music and a cheerful weather man who went on and on about the marvellous sunny day it was going to be and how all the trains to Brighton and Southend were going to be on time, and wasn't that nice? There wasn't a hint there had been a war.

Then I found a station that had just started up.

"This is the voice of the Midlands Committee," a voice with a strong Birmingham accent was saying. "Using BBC equipment we intend to provide an honest and objective service for those trapped inside the infected area. Since it is anticipated that efforts by both the British and Red Armies will be made to silence us we are initially broadcasting for only a quarter of an hour at a time starting on the hour. The signal after this broadcast will be very much weaker since we will be broadcasting from mobile equipment and immediately changing our location. Army listeners, please take note, to save aviation fuel.

"Now down to business," the voice continued. "If you have been listening to the regular government broadcasts from both sides you will realise that they have forged a conspiracy to pretend that nothing ever happened. At this moment both governments have begun to build a fence to enclose the whole infected area. Thus we will be sealed in. When this is achieved we shall be even more at their mercy. It is important therefore that those of us who have survived, most of us teenagers, become prepared for all eventualities. First, however, we must stop the gang rivalry that has broken out. This helps no one but the soldiers and politicians who caused this conflict. Responsible people in the Birmingham region are therefore invited to a grand meeting, time and location to be announced tomorrow and the necessary security arrangements. Come! The more the merrier!

"Before we close down – I have just been informed that fighter-bombers have crossed the M5 flying in the direction of Pebble Mill – here are some facts we have gleaned. The disease is expected to remain infectious for a minimum of two hundred years. If, however, you have survived you are immune. No more worry: the common cold poses a more vicious threat. Outsiders, however, are not so lucky. If they have not already been exposed to the disease their chances of dying are ninety-five per cent. This is certainly likely to be true of children born to us, though obviously no one knows for sure as yet.''

Without warning the station went off the air.

At that moment Alex appeared with another boy. Today they were using the car. They inched it out into the road, drove it up and parked on the drive of one of the houses. I settled down on the balcony as they carried stuff out to the car, took it back down the hill, then carried out more and moved on to the next house.

Nine o'clock passed – ten o'clock – eleven. Alex and his helper were on their fourth house by now. They were slaving away as if it were a race against time.

At a quarter past eleven I decided it was time to tackle Alex. I took courage and left the flats. I ran across the grass towards Budge's road. There was a tarmacked way for cars from the flats, but I ran up the side of a house and settled in a place from which I could see but not be seen.

What temptation there was to walk across, plonk myself in front of Alex and say "Here I am," to get it over with. But what would I say next? How could I tempt him away? Why should he be tempted? And why should I want to tempt him so badly? Our friendship had ended some time ago. Was there any chance it could be resurrected? I know now there wasn't but that morning loneliness must have gnawed at me like a rat in my innards.

At about twelve o'clock Alex and the other boy brought the car out on to the road with the back seat full to the roof. Alex jumped out of the driving seat to shut the gate.

"You drive it down," he called. "I want to scout round.

I'll eat up here. Bring it back in half an hour."

"What will Budge say?" the other boy protested.

"You can drive it?"

"Of course I can!"

Alex gave the car a thump. "Drive it then. When you come back, wait here. I'll keep an eye out."

"But what about Budge?" the boy insisted.

"I'm in charge of the house-to-house collecting. Do as you're told." He walked across to the gate of the garden I was hiding in. He opened it then shouted, "Get on with it, then! I'm having a look round here. Go on!" The car jerked away.

Alex came through the gate and closed it behind him. "All right, Darren. I saw you earlier. Where are you hiding?"

I went cold. I didn't reply.

"I'm not armed, if that's what you're worried about," he said after a moment. "I saw you were. The advantage is yours. Come on – hurry up before someone comes to see what I'm up to. Budge has a suspicious mind."

I stepped out of my hiding-place, heart thumping. Alex swung round to face me. He eyed my axe.

"So you got left behind too," he said. "I had that feeling." He scanned my face. "What do you want? To join us?"

I shrugged. After all this time was that the first thought that sprang to his mind?

"He's got a grudge and a half against you," he said eyeing my axe again. "But I could probably bring him round."

"I don't think I need to join," I said.

"You're on your own?" Alex asked. I nodded automatically and immediately kicked myself for having let that slip. "On your own you're a target for anyone," Alex insisted. "You ought to see what's going on further into Birmingham. Budge and I drove in there, Bearwood way, last night. We were lucky to get away with our lives. One guy appeared from round the corner when we stopped to have a look and threw a grenade at us. The idiot forgot to pull out the pin!"

Fascinated by this Alex who appeared to have grown up so

quickly I asked, "What did you do?"

"Pulled out the pin and chucked it back of course!"

"You got him?"

"Yeah," Alex said, swaggering. "Pity I didn't ask him where he got it from first."

I didn't know what to say. I looked at him goggle-eyed. Alex got me wrong. He coloured and looked away.

"Okay, this lunatic threw something at us. He was screaming like God knows what. We thought it was a grenade. Budge shot him."

I swallowed. "And Budge?"

"What about him?"

"How is he?" I felt idiotic inquiring after his health when I wished him dead. This was going all wrong.

"Fine. We're really sorting things out. We make a good team."

Good team – him and Budge? That bully? I felt choked up. It was so unreal.

"Where are you staying? Still in the house?" Alex asked.

I managed to lie. "I moved up in the estate near the shops. I found a really comfortable place. There's a gang up there. I've got friendly."

"Them – " Alex said contemptuously. "Those – " he spat.

Suddenly I glanced at the road, thinking I heard footsteps. Mightn't this be a trap? Alex seemed so cold.

"You want me to take you down to Budge?" he asked, eyeing the axe again. I gripped it tight. Wouldn't Budge be pleased if he took me back – better than a lorryload of food any day! Was that what was in his mind?

"How can you stand him?" I burst out. "He's a creep and a bully and a sadist. He'd stab you in the back as soon as look at you if it suited him. You've sold yourself!"

"Look – I've survived this far and I aim to survive a lot longer," Alex said fast and furious and contemptuous. "How well do you think you're going to manage on your own?" He sneered. "Turn down my offer and you'll be back soon enough begging Budge and me to take you in." It was "Budge and me" now. "You either survive or you don't – there's no in between."

"You and me – " I said, "we could do a lot better than this – " I gestured at the road. "You know we could. Don't you remember – "

"Oh here it comes," he said. "Dreams! What is it today? Famous Five or Secret Seven? Is that why you're dogging me?" He turned away.

"Wait!" I called. "Please."

He stopped in mid-stride.

"I don't owe you anything, Darren," he said. "Get that straight. That night Budge and I found the car in your road, you were there, weren't you? Just thank your lucky stars Budge didn't know. He hates you."

"Then go and tell on me."

"If I need to I can deal with you myself," he said. "Don't you think otherwise. And I will if you get in my way."

I turned my back. I had tears in my eyes I didn't want him to see.

Suddenly I heard Alex on the gravel. I swivelled and glimpsed his body launched at me. His head crunched against my hip. Then we were both lying winded on the ground.

I crawled out of his grasp and knelt, scrabbling for the axe which had flown out of my hand. I got it. Alex was just getting to his feet. He came at me again and grabbed me round the waist. We swayed together.

"You stuck up bastard – with your whining father – and your little spoiled bitch of a sister – what was her name?" We wrestled and he mouthed in my ear. "She's copped it, has she? I'm glad. She deserved it. And your patronising father – share our food, Alex – come as often as you like, Alex – then send you to another school to keep me away. I hope you had to bury him with your own hands."

I went mad and swung the axe, hitting him with the flat.

He staggered way.

"I'm sorry, Darren. I didn't mean it. I didn't, honestly." Alex kept backing away and away. God! was he scared of me! I followed him. He was blubbering. I hit him again and was glad. I hated him as much as he hated me.

9

That night I slept as peaceful as a lamb, the sleep of the just.
The war, the bomb, the disease, the fence, Budge, the gang
– they might never have been. My triumph over Alex
obliterated them all. If this person I'd loved before the bomb
was now my deadly enemy, so what? Hatred was what life
was all about. Fighting the Russians, storming the fence –
these actions didn't even occur to me. But hate Alex with all
my passion – I could do that.

That night I felt inoculated against fear. If a relationship
ended, did it have to turn into hatred? It did. I knew it did.
Alex had said what Dad's reasons were for making me go
to that other school – they weren't reasons Dad had given
to me, but had he had them in mind? Perhaps Dad had merely
tolerated Alex. I'd misinterpreted the way he'd felt – all my
jealousy had been misplaced.

The next day I stayed on though I'd meant to go but
the revenge expedition didn't come. Alex seemed to have
believed me about moving on. Two days, three, I continued
to court fate. Then I grew bolder, breaking into neighbour-
ing houses. No one seemed to claim the territory. Perhaps
I was just lucky. Or was Alex biding his time, waiting to

take his revenge? How had he explained his beating to Budge though?

But soon anxiety grew again. I couldn't see myself ever making Budge scared, not even the hard new me. For him I'd always be Fatso. While Budge was around I'd be Fatso to myself.

I went from elation to deep depression. I re-lived the way he had beaten me up those nights after school at the bus stop. I remembered the relief I'd felt the night Dad had appeared out of the blue. Ten seconds before Budge had become aware of his imminent arrival and tried to run away, I too had glimpsed Dad out of the corner of my eye. I'd managed to land a ferocious blow on Budge's mouth, the kind of blow that till that psychological moment I'd been temperamentally incapable of. Then it had all seemed like the end of a bad dream, but the bad dream had now come back. It would have been better if he had gone on beating me up till he'd grown tired of the game and found other victims.

Four mornings after my fight with Alex I was woken early. It was the gang coming up the cul-de-sac, with Alex in the lead, an enormous bandage over the top of his head, two boys behind him, then Budge carrying a gun and two other boys bringing up the rear. I'd been wrong. Alex was after all going to exact his revenge this way. Yet no one even gave my home a second glance except Alex who eyed it surreptitiously. The six passed straight up the road and out of sight, led by that bandaged head.

I got dressed and went after them. Near the top of Keats Avenue I saw them again. There were shouts ahead, then a single gun shot. I plunged into a garden and ran up the side of the house where I'd seen one go. Round the back I nearly stumbled over a boy but he was too intent on the battle to notice me. I dodged down behind a coal-bunker.

Budge had caught the shop gang out on a shopping expedition. The fronts of the two shops – the newsagent's and the grocery store – had had the boards removed. The shop gang must be inside.

Budge was crouched behind a wall with the gun. Nothing happened for ages. I crouched behind the coal-bunker, not daring to move. I was stuck since I didn't want to be spotted by either side.

Then suddenly Budge was shouting.

"You've got two minutes!" he bawled. "Then we're coming in to get you. Throw out your weapons and come out with your hands above your heads. We won't harm you."

In front of me Budge's men squirmed about. I ducked right down. When I dared to peer over the coal bunker again Budge had his gun trained over the top of the wall in the direction of the shop. No one came out.

He didn't give any warning when the two minutes were up but suddenly fired twice. Whether he hit what he intended to I don't know. The results were dramatic enough in their way. The sign above the newsagent's fell sideways and began to swing. The boarding rattled. Still no one appeared. Budge reloaded. He didn't shoot again. More stalemate and, it appeared, the end of the negotiations.

Then a cautious figure began to slide along the side of the shops. This figure carried a milk bottle. A milk bottle? What kind of weapon was that? I soon found out. He put it down and was fumbling with something. Matches. He picked up the bottle and slung it against the boards. There was a bang and they erupted into flames. The bottle appeared to bounce back. The boy became enveloped in flames as well. He burned and screamed, twisting this way and that trying to escape.

The front of the shops was now well ablaze. First one figure, then another, came running out. Budge shot down two of them. His aim was spot on. He quickly reloaded and fired again. I fancied that in the confusion he shot down his own blazing torch of a man. Probably it put him out of his misery. It turned out that one of the shop people had got away, a boy, not the man. I didn't see the man. The shops and their contents burnt merrily.

I waited in the house. I should have gone by now but my will seemed paralysed.

No one came back down the cul-de-sac. Probably Budge's gang was digging in to their captured territory.

I made myself eat and tidied up round the house. The evening came, shadows lengthened. The air grew slightly chilly. It was going to be a fine clear night. I couldn't rest.

About nine I went out and locked up. I set off down towards the bridge, meaning to have another look at Budge's road. What I hoped to achieve by that I had no clear idea. However instead I turned left along the stream and then out into the middle of the park, away from the stream and its concealing trees. At that time of night, in that darkness, with just the light of the stars – it may not have been a particularly brave thing to do but I felt very foolhardy. I turned up the slope and began to climb.

It was a steep grassy bank where we used to sledge in winter and I was out of breath by the time I reached a level shelf of grass, a hundred metres up. I looked back into the valley. It was misty down in the bottom. On the far side of the stream there had once been coal pits, and by the stream itself blast furnaces had stood which made the whole area gleam at night – so Dad had said. There wasn't a gleam of light tonight, not even on the hillside beyond where there were more streets of houses.

I went on climbing. There were trees now, in clumps, with paths running between them. Then from my left and above me I heard a faint sound.

I became frozen to the spot. I couldn't move backwards or forwards. I had to force myself to move to find out what the noise was. I glided on to the grass and went towards the sound up the bank. It got louder and before I saw what made it I suddenly recognised where I was. Where the ground levelled out again there was a children's playground, swings and roundabouts and climbing frames. I smiled to myself. It was only a swing shifting in the breeze.

I couldn't have been more wrong. The playground was peopled. Perched on the swings and roundabouts were seven or eight figures, with hoods over their heads like monks, absolutely silent. The only sound was the faint creaking of the swing. Figures more ghostly than ghosts, waiting for me to blunder into them.

A cigarette end glowed in the dark.

"Might as well die of cancer as anything else," a voice said. "Think they'll airlift in more?"

"Best not to get addicted," another voice said. "No use relying on them."

"They can't just leave us," a third voice objected. "It stands to reason."

"I wouldn't bet on it," the second voice said. "Not if you go by what the radio from Birmingham says."

No one said anything after that.

I didn't move. I was attracted by this circle of humans. In the end I crouched down. They were unlikely to see me from where they were. If anyone came my way I could run, and I would run away from the direction of home to give them a false trail.

And then I suddenly recognised the hoods. They were wearing anoraks from the general store next to the newsagent's. The Pakistani shopkeeper had been selling them cheap all last winter. The breeze was blowing on my back. I could have done with an anorak myself.

"The guy who was leading you, the one that got shot, what was he like?" a voice asked.

I'd not thought about this; Budge must have recruited the remnants of the shopping-centre people.

"He wouldn't let us out of his sight," a voice grumbled. "All that estate to go looking through and he wouldn't let us out of that road. A lot of good it did him."

"He was right," Alex's voice said suddenly, but I couldn't see which figure he was. "This stuff's got to last us. It's all we've got. I went up that block of flats near our road. You can see miles from there. You can see right to the motorway. They're building the thickest, highest fence ever put up by man. All to keep us in. The fewer they have to keep the better."

Everyone was listening to his older, authoritative voice. You could have heard a pin hit the ground.

"The people won't let them leave us here," an apologetic voice protested eventually.

"They won't have any choice. Who's got the power? Our government. The Reds. They know exactly what the stuff they dropped on us can do. Our side had it as well, don't you worry. Do you think they're going to be sentimental about us? It's their own necks they're worried about, not ours."

"We're people still," the voice answered Alex.

"We're us now," Alex said, "that's all. Lepers. We're on our own. No one's responsible for us. What did they ever do for the survivors of the Eighties Blitz? Well?" No one answered him. "Shot them, thousands of innocent Germans."

Unconsciously I had been creeping forward till I was quite close to the hooded figures draped over the slides and climbing frames. I could see Alex now, the bandage making his head bulky. It was he who was making the swing squeak. I knew what he said was right.

I was almost on the point of standing up and going forward when another voice spoke up. "Alex – that bandage round your head. You never really told us how you came to get attacked."

"No, you haven't," several other voices said.

"Who was he? Didn't you see him?"

"I got a glimpse."

"Would you know him again?"

"Maybe," Alex said. "Don't worry – I'll get my own back one day, twice over."

Another voice chipped in.

"Someone broke into the newsagent's once. The 'Man' went in and tackled him."

"Mr Rafferty," another voice added.

"Oh, and what happened?" Alex asked with interest.

"He let him go. He was someone from down the bottom of the estate. He was real soft, the 'Man'. I would have shot him."

"Perhaps it was the same person," Alex said softly. "But there's no one down the bottom of the estate now. He'll turn up though."

I could tell from the tone of his voice he knew I was still there. A shiver passed up my spine. It was as if he knew I was listening to him at that moment.

Then there were footsteps on the road that led to the park gates. The gathering stiffened. Several figures slipped off the frames and stood loosely to attention.

Budge stopped just inside the gates. He gave orders.

"The ones who joined today, plus Alex, and John, come with me – the rest go to the house by the shops. Simon's there. He's in charge. You do what he says. Come on, jump to it!"

"All right, Budge?" Alex said easily. He leaped off the swing and stood by Budge's side.

"Fine," Budge said. "Done well, haven't we?" He clapped Alex on the shoulder.

They marched off down the road. Clip-clop, clip-clop. They were kitted out in heavy boots. The Pakistani shopkeeper had done a good trade in them too.

When they'd gone I ran, letting the hill take me. Far to my right I could hear the boots clip-clopping, the night's only sound.

10

A lull. That brief burst of murderous violence, then seemingly nothing. I stayed for two days in the house before venturing out again. After that I went into the park more and more often, up to the swings. Occasionally I heard a car roaring about the estate, but no one bothered me. No one I saw came through our cul-de-sac. They seemed to prefer another route to the second base which I assumed they'd established near the shops. I didn't know. I only went once into the estate.

That time I scouted along the road down which Budge had marched his army and I broke into a house through a back window.

Its downstairs was full of useless gadgetry – dish washer, computer, video – the lot. I tested the settee in front of the television. I was dog-tired with forever being on guard. I began to drift off to sleep. Then suddenly it occurred to me that it ought to be possible to get a generator going and use all of this. There must be literally hundreds of generators in the factories and depots in the area, and millions of gallons of fuel beneath garage forecourts. Even if they were sealed off from me now, as if they were still beneath the North Sea, they need not be for ever. There must be some way of finding out how they worked.

I climbed out of the house, whatever purpose I'd had when I'd broken in forgotten. The street was clear. I set off back home through the park. The future. There *was* a future. I knew where there was a car I thought I could get started. One more night around here and I'd go.

It was this elation that made me careless returning home. I didn't keep a proper look-out. If I hadn't prolonged my walk and approached the house from below, from the park, the direction they didn't expect me in, I'd have been caught. For, whether Alex had at last deliberately come looking for me or they'd searched the house on one of their expeditions, they must have found I was living there. I could see figures in the back garden rifling through a pile of things from my house and the Homers'.

I dodged back into the shelter of the trees by the stream. Budge came storming out and shouted at his underlings. His words didn't carry to me but the Cortina was out in front and I saw it being filled with our things. It came and went twice before evening. I crept up into Sally's tree-house and stayed there. By evening, even though I didn't detect any movement up in the cul-de-sac I didn't go to check. They might have been lying in wait. I had the axe. That was all that I was left with and could take with me. It was ridiculous hanging about any longer. I would definitely leave tomorrow. There was now no reason to stay.

I slept amazingly well, up in the tree. I woke a couple of times to see the stars in the sky above me – then went back to sleep. I was finally woken by the sound of a gunshot. I scrambled up. There was the sound of another shot. It came from the direction of Budge's street.

A quarter of an hour later I was at my vantage point on the balcony at the top of the block of flats. The room had been trampled through and other doors on the stairs had been broken in.

WE'LL GET YOU NEXT TIME, FATSO

had been scrawled across one of the lounge walls and
YOU PEEPING TOM.

Another set of graffiti described exactly what was the excruciating death in store for me. It seemed too well spelt to be Budge's handiwork.

It was easy to see what was happening. Budge and Alex had discovered that someone was living in the boarded-up house with the window ajar. My instinct had been right.

I left the flats and ran home. It was my chance to salvage what they'd left, if they'd left anything, and make off. I could try and get the car I knew about, too. The distraction of the siege would give me time. I hadn't yet worked out where to go. Into the country probably. If I'd understood properly there was plenty of that this side of the Fence. Ultimately I meant to find the people who ran the radio. They sounded sane. Oddly enough, I hadn't given a thought to the person who was under siege.

I ran past BUDGE RULES THE WORLD, down past the factory, over the bridge and up the path into the end of the cul-de-sac. I plunged in through the open back door.

They'd wrecked the house. Everything they hadn't removed they'd torn, cut, broken or defaced. The walls were covered with messages, all directed at me. When I'd taken in the mess in the kitchen I walked slowly through the downstairs rooms and then went upstairs. Anger like a great big sob welled up in me. Why such hatred? Why me? The longer I stayed the less able I was to comprehend it. It seemed to have nothing to do with me, even if I was the target. Dad would have said to pity them for their being this way. I couldn't. I hated them.

I went back to the end of Budge's road and walked up it. There was a sharp bend to the left with houses high on a bank. The garages were at street-level, cut into the front gardens. I could just see the roof of the shuttered house. I climbed up the steps to one of the other houses and began to make my way through the gardens.

There was a hedge between the shuttered house and me. I parted the leaves. Budge with the gun and Alex were standing in front of the house, two others just behind them. Two of the upstairs windows had been blown in through the shutters.

A girl appeared at one of the windows. She was a breath-takingly pretty girl. Budge just stood and looked at her. My heart stopped a second.

"Being sensible? Opening that door, are you?" he said.

"I'll see you dead first," the girl called back, more furious than scared. She undid the catch of the window and pushed it full open.

"Got a ladder anyone?" Budge said. "Alex?" He suddenly lifted the gun and fired. The brickwork above the window showered down dust as the bullet struck it. The girl ducked, picked something up and threw. It was a heavy-looking bottle which struck the ground by his feet and cracked. He was showered with liquid and broken glass. Budge seemed to enjoy it, he didn't even seem unnerved. He shouted back, "You'll pay for that!" as if it were a joke. The girl had something else in her hand but Budge had lifted the gun and was pointing it directly at her. She hesitated then dropped below the level of the window sill. Budge fired through the window. You could hear the bullet ricochet about the room. He handed the gun to one of the boys behind him for reloading.

"Right, Anna darling! That's your name, isn't it? I remember you. The game's over. You've hidden yourself away long enough. I'm coming to get you. I'm counting to ten."

Budge began to count.

I hoped fervently the girl would have the sense to make her get-away out of the back of the house, until I remembered there may have been more members of the gang round there.

"Nine ... eight ... seven ... six." Budge savoured each number. "What comes next, Anna? Ah yes, five ... still there, are you? Got left behind by Mummy and Daddy, did you? Three ... two ... one and a half ... we're coming to get you,

Anna ... one and a quarter ... your last chance, Anna ... Anna ...one ...'' He grabbed the gun back off his bearer and fired in through the centre window again. No zero. Then he shot again.

The moment after the second shot Anna re-appeared at the window and threw another of the heavy objects she seemed so well provided with. This time she hit Budge in the chest. He gasped and sank to the ground. Of the others only Alex stood his ground. He grabbed the gun and reloaded it. Something whistled past his ear. Alex took aim at the girl, but didn't fire. She ducked out of sight.

"Come back, you cowards!" Alex shouted at the two by the gate. He turned the gun towards them. He leant down and pulled at Budge's arm. "Budge! Get up! Don't just lie there!"

Budge struggled to all fours. "I'll get you, you cow, if it's the last thing I do!" he screamed at the house. "You'll wish you'd never thrown that."

The four whispered by the gate. It didn't take much to see that if one went round the back of the house to join whoever else was there they couldn't fail to get in.

Eventually they did just that. Alex edged past the garage down the side of the house out of my sight. Budge stood facing the house, his gun ready, a subordinate at each side. They waited a pace back from him.

What was I supposed to do? I couldn't just leave the girl to her fate, but I'd been going, hadn't I? I'd had enough. What was this girl to me? My anger had become more reasonable, Budge seemed invincible.

There was a piercing whistle from the back. The gang at the front launched into a series of blood-curdling war cries. Budge fired twice into the top window. His side-kicks threw what they could find, though all three still kept a respectful distance from the house.

I left my place of safety and headed for the back of the house. I didn't bother about any noise I might make.

They couldn't possibly hear me above their own screams and shrieks.

At the back the gardens were separated by a waist-high fence. I knelt behind my last piece of cover and peered over to see what was happening. A rather sheepish-looking lad was there with Alex. They had found a ladder in a shed at the bottom of the garden. It was just long enough to reach to the first floor window level. The windows on the ground floor were boarded up, but not those upstairs. Alex was at the top of the ladder, a brick in his hand preparing to smash a pane of glass. The other youth was on the bottom of the ladder, gazing around nervously.

I didn't hesitate but jumped straight over the fence brandishing my axe. The ladder-steadier tumbled off the bottom rung and backed away from me along the wall. Alex yelled, tottered, regained his balance by grabbing at the window sill, glanced down furiously and saw me.

All this time war cries were coming from the front. I didn't know whether to follow the frightened one, who was getting away, or whether to tackle Alex. Alex partly solved that question by dropping the brick at me instead of smashing the window. Luckily his aim was wildly out. Enraged by the brick I struck at the side of the ladder with all my force. The ladder wasn't planted very firmly and swivelled crazily on one leg. With a yelp Alex tumbled off.

He landed close to me. For a second time I had him at my mercy. I could have knocked him unconscious, maimed him, killed him, anything. But something held me back and Alex saw it in my eyes. He scrambled up.

"Go away, Darren!" he said. He was appealing to me. "She's mine. I mustn't let Budge get his hands on her." For a fraction of a second I was insanely jealous. I don't know what stopped me from striking him with the axe. At the same time I was without mercy. I shook my head. "You can come with us," he said. I thought of the girl, strong, beautiful in that window. "You and me and Anna."

"I'm giving you two seconds, Alex," I said. I steadied the axe. "Don't think I wouldn't use it."

Alex turned tail.

I stood there utterly confused. I began to realise my foolishness in having let him go.

"Hide!" a voice from above hissed. I glanced up. The girl was at an open window. "Quick! They'll be round in a minute. Go on! Hide!" she insisted. "Get away! I can manage them!" She made it sound as if she could. She slammed the window shut.

I ran and clambered into the next garden away from the direction I'd come from. It was full of bushes and small trees. I found a place to hide. None too soon. The gang came streaming after me.

11

"With an axe?" Budge was saying. "But we've a gun, haven't we!" I could see and hear perfectly from my hiding place. He began pointing the gun about in all directions as if expecting me to jump out at any moment, but he hadn't a lot to fear. My berserk fit had long passed.

The others ducked and weaved out of the way as the gun pointed towards them. "You load of babbies!" Budge said. "Except for her, he's on his own." He jerked the gun in the direction of the upstairs windows. "If he had any sense he would have climbed up to join her." He laughed. "But she probably didn't want him. Who can blame her."

"Let me have the gun," Alex said. "I can shoot straighter than you. He must be close. I heard her telling him to hide. Give it here." The sheepish youths nodded in agreement, then wished they hadn't when Budge turned on Alex.

"I keep it."

"I thought we were in this together," Alex said. "What happens when some gang comes scavenging over here from Harborne or Blackheath? There are more like us. We should all be able to use the gun when necessary. It's not just yours."

"The gun stays with me," Budge said, then ignored him.

"We've got to search," he said. He surveyed the garden. "The shed. Is he in the shed?" He raised his voice. "Are you there, Fatso? I know you can hear me. In the shed, are you?"

"Only if he's daft," Alex said and turned away. "And he didn't use to be."

"He's rattled you, hasn't he?" Budge said. Light glimmered. "Was it him bashed you over the head?"

"Shut up," Alex said, "and get on with it." He turned back to Budge ferociously.

"Jumped you, did he? Got his own back on his old mate? Or were you thinking of palling up with him again?"

"Idiot!" Alex said in a rage. "Give me the gun or get on with it."

Budge gave him a long appraising look then prodded one of the sheepish ones. "You go and look."

"Why me?"

"*Go!*" Budge swung his gun in the boy's direction.

A mad axe-man in the shed, Budge with a gun behind him. No wonder the boy looked close to tears as he made his way up the garden. He stopped short of the shed, then, inspired, went and peered in through the window. "He's not here," he shouted.

"Look inside, you coward!" Budge shouted. "He's probably crouched down. Aren't you, Fatso?"

The boy made a quick calculation then ran round the back of the shed. "Come back here!" Budge shouted, advancing. "I'm warning you!" The boy made another sudden rush and jumped over the hedge into the garden where I was and ran like a madman for the end. He scrambled over the fence and disappeared into the coppice of trees that lay behind it. I suddenly realised they were the trees on the top of the bank behind the factory. I was actually quite near home. Budge cursed and fired at his retreating ex-private but merely managed to chip wood out of the fence.

Then there were only four, Budge and Alex half-smirking, and the two remaining half-hearted ones. "I won't miss you!"

Budge promised as they looked longingly in the direction their friend had taken. That made me wonder. There ought to have been far more of them. What *had* happened to the others? Had they deserted?

Alex swung on Budge. "Right, there's been enough of this fooling about ..."

"Quieter! He can probably hear us," one of the sheepish ones said.

"You're right," Alex said, drawing them all into a huddle in the middle of the lawn. After a couple of minutes they'd worked something out. The two half-hearted ones were posted at the corners of the house. Budge and Alex, Alex carrying the ammunition, began to walk round the edges of the garden.

They started by the spot I'd jumped over and shot into the bushes to make sure I hadn't gone back there. They worked up all that side, firing three shots into spots they couldn't see well – they were taking no risks with my axe. Then they came back and started all over again on the side I was. They came towards me, peering and firing. Soon they were more or less opposite my hiding-place, which was about five metres from the fence.

I could no longer see them as well as I would have liked. They seemed to linger longer than usual examining the area I was in.

"Is this where you've been disappearing at nights?" I heard Budge ask Alex under his breath.

"What do you mean?"

"This girl. That's what I mean."

"I haven't disappeared anywhere at nights."

"Oh yes you have. Last night and the night before. Other nights for all I know. Were you in there with her?"

"I was just scouting around. I told you."

"We said it was share and share alike." Did Budge sound hurt? Aggrieved?

"With you first choice as usual?" Alex said.

"So you have been here before."

"I told you. I spotted her last night."

"Then why did someone else have to tell me?"

"Drop it!"

"Or was it her knocked you over the head? Hey, look – !"

Budge fired. The shot singed my shoulder. I clapped my hand to the spot and found it had taken a chunk out of my T-shirt.

Alex saw me too. "Another!" he shouted. "We've got him!" I jumped up and began to run. I weaved from left to right among the shrubs. I heard the crack of the gun. I swear the bullet passed between my knees.

They've got to reload I told myself. I could hear someone thumping after me through the garden. There were shouts from further back.

"Stay there! Watch her!"

"Come on, Budge!" That was Alex shouting.

I scrambled on to the fence, fell over it, picked myself up and ran down the path that greeted me. It went into the trees, then bore left along the contours of the hill. I'd no idea where it would take me. All I knew was that the coppice was sand-wiched between the houses on the lane and the factory by the bridge. I stumbled in and out of a pot-hole and sprawled full-length. Alex was calling, "He went this way."

My ankle hurt as I crawled to my feet. I tried to run but couldn't. "Ready," I heard Budge say a few metres away, snapping something shut. "No wonder they practise all the time in the Army." I ran on all-fours into the bushes looking for somewhere to conceal myself. I dived beneath some bushes as the two reached the place where I'd stumbled. They didn't even glance my way. They passed out of sight. Soon I couldn't even here their voices.

My ankle hurt more and more as peace descended on the coppice. I crawled further into the bushes and found a small clearing in the middle of them. I stood up and tested my ankle. It was wobbly, but getting better. I sat and waited and mas-saged it. Budge and Alex hadn't come back. I had time to think. What was I doing here, risking my life for a girl I'd never even seen before, except as a shadow? One who seemed to be able to stick up for herself perfectly well? One moreover with some hazy connection with Alex? How his eyes had pleaded when I'd had him at my mercy at the house. Forget that. I wondered where he and Budge had got to. I supposed by now they would be lying in wait for me at my house. But I didn't need to go back there. I'd said my farewells.

But then it came to me. It was either me or Budge. I couldn't live around here with Budge on the loose but this was where I came from and why should I go anywhere else? It was the same for Budge. He had to eliminate anyone who was against him, not just for his own safety but also to keep face with his gang – or what was left of it.

Another area would have its own Budge. Hadn't this turned into a Budge's world? It was him or me. Kill Budge or be killed.

I agonised for half an hour or more before the two appeared on the path again. They were moving along more stealthily. However they didn't catch me out. They went past.

I waited another half hour. There were no sounds from the direction of the girl's house, no shouting or gunshots, but I had to take my chance sooner or later even though I didn't entirely trust the pair to have left the coppice.

I crawled down through the bushes. I came to another very narrow path which I scurried over into more bushes. On hands and knees I crawled under them, then when the bank became steep turned round on to my backside and went feet first to save my ankle. I was being scratched to pieces. Below me was the wall of the factory. Across the factory's other side, a quarter of a mile away, I could see where the road ran. I slithered to the foot of the wall and stood up.

The wall was easy enough, though high, but as I sat on the top, poised to drop over, a shot whizzed past me. There was a crack as the branches of a tree at the top of the bank broke and a disgusted call from Alex of "You missed him again!"

I dropped from the wall, hobbled across a car park and disappeared from their view among the maze of factory buildings. I knew there was a gap in the fence by the stream about fifty metres down from the bridge – or at least there had been one a couple of years ago where I used to get into the factory grounds when it was deserted on Sundays.

I hurried, limping badly, between the buildings, bearing left towards the stream. I found myself in a long avenue that led towards the main gates. The gates were a hundred metres off when I was fired on again. The shot ricocheted off the step of a building on my left – I noticed CANTEEN on the door. At the end of the canteen I turned left. I was in a row of buildings nearest the stream. Where was that gap? It had been so long ago. Hidden – yes. Behind what? I looked right and left desperately. There were bicycle sheds with sagging corrugated roofing, leaning in a sea of weeds. The gap was behind them. I tried to sprint, feeling my ankle about to give way at any time. I stumbled through the weeds, pushed past brambles at the back of the shed and found the gap was still there. I could hear Alex and Budge shouting to each other. They seemed to have split up. I squeezed through the gap and bore right along the narrow bank towards the bridge. It was hard going, overgrown with crumbly soil underneath.

I heard Budge come out through the fence. I ran on, my left foot more in the water than out of it. Then I stopped. I'd made a terrible mistake. I should have gone left. Alex had appeared ahead of me. He'd found another gap between me and the bridge. He grinned – was it with relief that at last I'd been caught, or was it just pure pleasure at having hunted me down?

Budge started shouting, "Got him! Got him!" between gasps of exhaustion. As he and Alex converged on me he checked his gun and took aim. I went into the water. There was no escape on the other side – only a high grey concrete wall topped with wire netting and behind it tanks for flood water. The water was knee-deep and freezing cold. I remember

I was scared of drowning along with all the other ways I might have died. "Come on! Get it over!" Alex urged. "Budge! Budge!" I was almost opposite him now, though he made no move towards me. Budge had stopped and took final aim. I stopped too. Could you dodge bullets? I was almost too weary to care what happened.

The gun seemed to have jammed. Budge struggled with the trigger, his aim everywhere but directly at me. I began to wade towards him, brandishing my axe which I'd clutched all the while without thinking. I was suddenly aware of its power. Budge was terrified as I stepped out on to the bank two metres from him. I advanced holding the axe aloft. "Club him with the gun!" Alex screamed. "Don't just stand there, Christ!" Budge didn't hear him. He was too scared of me! He was too scared to do anything but grin and pump at the trigger. I wasn't Fatso any longer.

I reached him and struck. He put the gun up to defend himself but the blow of the axe struck it aside. The blade bit deep into his shoulder. He gasped. I lost hold of the axe which seemed to have a life of its own. It flew away. I closed with Budge and tried to wrestle the gun off him. The gun went off. There wasn't much left of his head when I stood back and looked at him.

PART THREE

Anna

Darren left two days ago for the Fence. How long he'll be gone I've no idea – you can wait days and days for a reply to the simplest request, or get one within minutes to something you were dubious about. Obviously this timing's deliberately part of the psychological hold they assert over us. At best it's creepy waiting for the answer to come up. You aren't allowed to question. One request, one answer. That's all you're allowed. It tends to cut out arguments.

I used to go down there with Darren once, but now he seems to want to go on his own. He's always glad to get back though.

Communication Centre V is by the crossroads below the Oldbury Hypermarket complex. It's a prefabricated hut they winched there under an enormous helicopter: kitchen, beds, a living room, electricity, the computer terminal. Every comfort in fact.

It's the waiting you know you'll have to put in that's worst. We waited five days once and we were only asking for a replacement generator. What could there have been sinister in that?

While you're there you really feel in No Man's Land. Completely at their mercy. You're reminded of the restrictions.

You feel like a caged animal that has to throw itself from one side of its prison to the other, even if our prison's a hundred miles wide. I remember reading once that serfs in the Middle Ages never travelled more than a few miles from their villages all their lives, never dreamt of doing otherwise. Sometimes I feel even more restricted than that.

Once when we were sleeping down there I had this dream, that it was a whole plot by them, them outside. They'd made it up. There was nothing wrong, no disease. It was all a vast experiment. I woke up with the truth ringing in my ears.

I got up excited and angry and went to the window. I tore the curtains apart. What did I expect? Them peeping in at us, laughing?

In any case, as you might expect, they have the last laugh. The world, at least this part of it, has been a lot more peaceful since they dropped their germ bomb. Friendship of the Reds and Western European people – they talk about it all the time on all the radios. Really cheerful. Peace treaties have been abolished. Peace has *started*. They imply it's the genuine article. The Reds have even stopped being snide about the Americans, just smug. They use the bomb they dropped on Leicester as a fearful example of what happens when people don't talk. For all we know their talk of Peace may be true. It just sounds unreal. On the other hand we may be on the better side of the Fence. It may be hell out there. Maybe the Reds are completely in control. Mind you, the planes that come over have RAF markings. On the other hand they may have taken over the RAF. Who cares? We're immune.

Having nothing else to do I go up to the attic window with the binoculars. I can see Communication Centre V from here. Two days ago a blue car was parked the other side of the prefab from Darren's. Now I can see neither car. They must have moved them. I don't know whether it's a good thing or not for Darren to have company. He hates it, and needs it. We've gone nearly three months at the moment without seeing anyone.

I have a friend over Belbroughton way. I say a friend. I could live without her. Perhaps I'll go and visit if Darren hasn't arrived back by tomorrow. I'll leave a note. He can come over and fetch me when he turns up.

Wherever he goes Darren carries the sub-machine gun. A firearm's a necessary precaution. There are still trespassers and intruders, though fewer and fewer as the years pass. But it's hardly the Wild West. The really crazed have more or less wiped themselves out, though every now and then something snaps in one of us apparently 'adjusted' citizens. Generally they broadcast a warning on the radio. 'Nutter on the loose.' Words to that effect. The winter after the bomb was the hardest time. Lots of the loners and loonies died then. A real weeding out. And anyone who made a habit of lurking about, posing a threat real or imaginary, inevitably got shot. Darren's killed a couple here, near the house: not recently though. I carry a pistol. I can shoot with it straight and I'm not always tripping over it.

Darren's got a thing about his gun. He eats with it propped against his chair, sleeps with it where the bedside lamp should be. However I think that on balance he's affected least of all the people I know by the precariousness of our position and how we got here. He's affected more by how he got left behind. For him the war ended the day we met.

When the gun went off in Budge's face and blew him to kingdom come Darren just made his way back to my house. Alex didn't bother him. He slipped away. We passed him on the road a month later when we were out in Dad's car reconnoitring for somewhere else to live. He just stepped to one side and looked at us – no emotion, just a stare. When those of us who wanted to live ordinary decent lives began to make contact and organised ourselves to deal with the gangs, we heard of him from time to time – in Hinckley at the head of some tearaways, later in the Solihull area living on his own and shooting at anyone who came near him, later still with

95

a girl in a cottage on Cannock Chase apparently settled down.

There's an odd thing I've picked up from what Darren wrote. (Oh yes, I read his memoirs the first time he left them with his last will and testament speech.) Why is it Darren's never directly told me in all the years we've been together that he knew Alex before? Because deep-down he believes Alex and I did have something going? Budge, yes – everyone in the district knew him, school children, school teachers, shop keepers, most adults. Everyone knew he was going to come to a sticky end – borstal, probation, or prison. Hanging won't be good enough for him they used to say. I was old enough by then to know the way he treated girls. But Alex was more terrifying in his way – so polite he was that morning I was careless by the window and he spotted me. If he'd brought a guitar and serenaded me flamenco-style at my balcony he couldn't have been more seductive and alluring. It was when I said no, for the nth time, you can't come in; I'm staying here till someone rescues me, sorry – nothing personal – you're not the one I had in mind, that he turned nasty. A switch in his mind flipped. Dirty bitch, cow, whore, all that. As if I was to blame for the war, for the germ bomb, for his having stayed behind with Budge for a lark. At least he told me it was for a lark.

But Darren and Alex. It's betrayal all over again. Darren betrayed by Alex, like his father betrayed him (or so he thinks). It makes me feel uneasy, jealous, as if I was second best. Darren rescued me to spite Alex because he'd gone with Budge. What if Alex after all had palled up with Darren? What would have happened to me then? It seems to give me a clue to a side of Darren that I don't want to know. I can accept that the carefree loving Darren is the same depressive who shivers in corners and doesn't speak for hours on end. I can accept the Darren who in Brownhills systematically stalked and eliminated the group of hooligans who had been terrorising our commune. Someone had to do it. But what gave him that peculiar intensity that's all Darren's own – his

'Darren-ness': Sally's death, his father's betrayal, killing Budge – was it there before, always there, blue-printed into his genes?

Darren and Alex: how similar they seem, two peas. Alex down in the garden under the window – "Let me in. I won't hurt you. I'll protect you. You need protection. There are gangs roaming about here. We'd make a good team, you and me together." And Darren coming back splattered with Budge's brains. What choice did I have but to let him in, my conquering hero, my protector? "Come in, Darren. God, what you've been through for me and we've not even been introduced." What was I supposed to say? "Dad bequeathed me a sub-machine gun. I know how to use it."

I wasn't like Darren. I didn't go wandering. I stayed at home.

Like Darren I came from a one-parent family, but unlike Darren I didn't have a brother or sister, and my mother wasn't dead but divorced from my father who brought me up. Probably my mother is still alive. She lived in Manchester which wasn't directly affected by the fighting or the disease. I've no way of telling, just as Darren has no way of telling about his dad. The Tripartite Government Commission that rules the Affected Zone (the A to Z as they call it sometimes on the radio with a wry affection) has a rule about not allowing survivors on different sides of the fence to know about one another. I think it's quite a good rule really. I wouldn't want the agony of knowing my loved ones were fenced away from me for ever. I'd rather live in doubt, which in this case is hope.

My dad was in the army and then ran a pottery shop in Birmingham. It did pretty well. It paid for that big house. He was a marvellous man. He gave me the courage to go on after he died. Darren doesn't like me to ask about his father because he won't talk about him, or his mother or Sally – but especially not about his father. I get the picture that they must have been a close-knit little family group, Sally rather dominating, the father rather opinionated and moody, loving but at the same time wrapped up in himself.

Darren hero-worshipped his father, in the absence of anyone else. I wonder if his father really drove Alex away. I don't think he did. And then his hero let Darren down, betrayed him utterly, in the way that heroes do. It must be a job living on a pedestal. Left them stranded, tied to the house with his promises to come back. So Sally died. So Darren got caged in here.

Of course we'll never know the truth, but Darren thinks he knows. Since the day Sally died he's always assumed the worst. His father had all the time in the world to get from Melton Mowbray or wherever it was but he never turned up. He's on the other side of the Fence now – Darren's convinced of it. He left them to find their own way to Wales, abandoned them, betrayed them.

I don't believe his father was the kind of man to do that. Nor does Darren, right down at the bottom of his heart. Perhaps the grief of believing he might be dead was too hard to bear.

I've never really questioned whether I love Darren or not. First there was nursing him back to health. Then deciding to leave for the city, finding others we could live at peace with, fighting to make sure we'd be left alone, finding this house high on a hill looking both into Birmingham and the countryside, fortifying it, our first dealings with the Tripartite Commission, the babies that died (as they said they would). Where has there been the luxury of time to think about whether I was forced to have him or not? Would I have loved him if there'd been no war and we'd still met? Or is that question just academic?

Last night, my third on my own, I couldn't get to sleep. The wind was howling outside. That's the only thing I don't like about this house – the way the slightest breeze up here acts like it's out to haunt someone. I thought I heard a car outside. I was pretty sure I did actually. Without lighting anything I went round to every peephole at every window. I didn't see anything even though it was a bright night.

Back in bed I started wondering about Alex. I wonder what kind of girl he's with, what she looks like, is she pretty or plain, do they get on all the time, have they managed to have children? Daft question. No one has.

I would have shot him if he and Budge had got in the house, but when he first came calling up to me how I wanted to let him in, how I wanted to trust him! I dream I did sometimes. I'm never sure how to react when I wake up and find I didn't.

Darren

Before I go into the TCCC (Tripartite Commission Communications Centre as it proclaims above the door) I get the petrol pump working and fill up. Then I turn the car round so it's facing the way I want to leave. Whenever I'm in a TCCC building I get the feeling I'm trapped and that two miles away, across the other side of the Fence a helicopter is about to take off. In a moment I'll hear it whirring above me, its machine-guns trained on the door. Sometimes that fear's so real my body tenses up so tight that five minutes later I find myself frozen to the spot like a statue.

I get out of the car and lock it for protection. I have my sub-machine gun at the ready and go up the steps into the building. There's a small entrance room. I notice nothing unusual. I'm a bit off my guard. I have been ever since leaving home. I push through the swing doors into the rest room and it hits me straightaway someone's been in here recently, there's an unwashed cup on the coffee table, things are out of place – everyone usually leaves it *exactly* as it was in here: it's a way of pretending we don't have to share the same space. Also there's the trace of a smell, not unpleasant but definitely the smell of another human being.

I feel the coffee cup. It's still warm. Gun at the ready I check all the rooms – the bedrooms, the bath, the toilet, the computer room. A window is unfastened in the second bedroom. I stand well back and gaze out. Then I see it – a car, parked among the trees two hundred yards away. The car's too far off for me to recognise it or its occupant. I can tell something about his or her character though – the driver's more furtive than me.

I fasten the window, then go in the computer room. I want this over with as quickly as possible with someone out there. The computer as usual fazes me. This one seems particularly bland and impersonal – no, hostile's the word. It reminds me in every square millimetre of its design, as if I needed reminding, that there's a thirty-foot fence all ready to burn me to a cinder if I set foot near it. It reminds me that I shall never in all my life be able to visit London or Edinburgh or Paris, or go to America or the South Pole or the Amazon Basin. It reminds me that sometimes I dream that they've turned the electricity off in their fence and I'm clean. I can gaze through the wires and far off, perhaps, I can see my father alive and well. He escaped, the bastard, and left Sally and me behind. The next day I'm a zombie. Anna works and talks around me and wonders. I can see her wondering what am I doing here with him? Why not someone else? Why not Alex, for example?

I identify myself to the computer, M8499 and type in my report that I have sighted a fox. I request live-stock to start an experimental small-holding. I ask that they deal with my request as quickly as possible. The screen says "WAIT" in big letters like that and ten minutes later it says "SOME DELAY IN ANSWERING YOUR REQUEST IS ANTICIPATED." Then I know I'm in for a long wait, as if I hadn't guessed already. I calculate. Will it be hours? Days?

I go into the bedroom and look for the car again. I see it driving off that moment, a blue family saloon. Not one I recognise. It slips among the trees and out of sight, in the direction of the road I came on.

Suddenly I make a decision. I will not wait for the computer's decision. I will come back for it. There are no rules that say you have to wait. There are no rules inside the Fence anyway, just sensible precautions.

Outside I rev the car and adjust the mirror so I can see the Fence. The air around it seems vaguely hazy. Is it imagination or not, does the immense current of electricity really charge the atmosphere, can electricity leak? I put the mirror back to its usual position and drive slowly away from the building. Where am I going? Home to Anna? I'm not sure. I raise my speed. The road's pot-holed and the car sways from side to side. At the crossroads I stop and let the engine idle. Straight on through the decaying towns, up the hill, along the lane? Why not? What have I got against it? I have the odd idea I'm off the hook today, I can go anywhere I want, I'm not accountable to anyone. Anna thinks I may be away days. I can get up to what I want. But things aren't like that, not this side of the Fence anyway. There's nowhere to go, nothing particular I want to get up to.

All the same I turn right. I find I'm heading elsewhere. I drive fast so I won't change my mind, criss-crossing through the maze of streets. I climb up the hill the way I came that day I tried to get Sally to Wolverhampton. I know the route through the town like the back of my hand. There's still evidence on the pavement all these years on of the car that went up in flames, the rusted subframe, shattered glass – someone appears to have found a use for the rest, I can't think what. I drop down the hill on the dual carriageway, turn right towards Solly Heath, turn left up its High Street on the reasonable assumption that the bus is still stuck under the bridge. Not long now and I'm driving into the estate, slowing down to turn into the cul-de-sac. The houses are a really sorry sight, wood rotten, paint peeled off, gutters and downpipes sagging or fallen off altogether, moss all over the brickwork. The roof of the house opposite ours has collapsed. And the weeds – waist deep!

I shut off the engine and get out. I'm not sure now. Do I really want to go in? I finger my key-ring – I still have my keys after all these years – and force myself up the ruined drive. I peer in through the front window like Budge and Alex did that night – everything looks the same as the last time I was here. I walk round the back and glance suspiciously at the door – as if my hate note would still be there after all these years!

I'm without my gun. Why I don't know. I'm not usually parted from it. Shall I fetch it from the car? I don't bother.

At last I find the courage. I pull my key-ring out and find the right key. It works. Miraculous. I let myself in. The kitchen stinks. I gaze at the table first where we always used to leave messages. But the table's as bare as I left it except for a layer of dust over the gouge marks Budge and Co. left on it. I run my hand over the wood, getting dirty, as if I doubt the evidence of my eyes. The hate messages are like new on the walls. Then I glance into the front room before going upstairs. Nothing's different, no one's even set foot in here since that day. The bathroom still smells to me of the shit they smeared it with. That has to be imagination. Coming downstairs I nearly fall head over heels. One of the steps has gone rotten under the carpet. Outside I lock the door, take the key off the key-ring and throw it as far as it will go. If only there were some evidence Dad had come back, I could forgive him then. Strange how you can become fourteen years old again, or for ever. Not strange – terrifying.

In the road, quickening my step, I glance towards the entrance to the cul-de-sac. There's a blue car standing there, blocking my exit. It's the car that was in the trees by the TCCC. I think briefly of bumping my own car down into the park and trying to outrun him that way, but I can see he's got his gun trained on me through the open passenger window.

I walk towards him, utterly defenceless.

Alex is completely mad. It's only by some fluke I'm going
to get out of this alive. He leaves the car. We have to walk
because he's got nothing to tie me up with. By pure chance
he was down at the TCCC this morning. That's how he came
to follow me. It's not far to walk anyway, wherever he's
taking me. The neighbourhood around here that matters to
us is very small.

Was he mad before going to the TCCC, or has seeing me
made him mad?

I worry about Anna. Does he know where we live? What
will he do to her if he kills me and gets hold of her? She's
good with the pistol though. Her bullet in his guts. There
would be a certain satisfaction in that.

As we walk along we chat, quite reasonably, as if he wasn't
holding a gun at my neck, as if something hadn't flipped in
his mind.

"A house in Bearwood overlooking the park," he tells me
when I inquire where he lives. It appears he's a bit of a DIY
maniac, the way he describes what he's done to this place.
All of us are more or less DIY experts since you can't just
flick through Yellow Pages and pick up the phone, but I
haven't come across an enthusiast before. He was down at
the TCCC, he tells me, to order some special materials for
a job he's got in hand. He's often down there, he says. The
computer's got a soft spot for him, he reckons, at least he
gets what he wants.

He's still mad, though, completely crackers, however
logically and tidily he's talking to me. He's got no reason to
be marching me along like this, no earthly reason.

I think he's changed precious little over the years. He's
clean-shaven, his face seems remarkably young, his hair's
thick, dark and strong. A picture of health. He's still got that
easy way I loved when I was ten.

I ask him, carefully, about the girl I heard he was living

with. He doesn't sound very enthusiastic, or perhaps it's just he's thinking about something else. He mentions they tried to have children. Like ours they were born with no immunity. They don't try any more. I think he means they don't make love any more. Anna and I go through phases like that.

We walk down past the end of the park, past the factory, up as far as the turning into Anna's road. BUDGE RULES THE WORLD shines as brightly as ever. "Good paint," I feel like commenting since he's a DIY nutter. I must be getting light-headed to feel so flippant.

"It's a pity we didn't keep it up," he says suddenly as we start to walk up the rise.

"What?" I say cautiously.

"Being friends," he says.

When? I wonder. When we changed schools, or that chance we had when he was looter-in-chief for Budge?

He tells me in a moment. "I was lost in that school without you," he says. "Whatever made your father send you up to that other place? It was cruel." He waits a moment, then he goes on. "I didn't mean it when I said he meant to split us up. Your dad was great. I liked him better than my own. Does that put it right?"

I paraphrase my answer. "Dad knew some of the teachers. He reckoned it would be easier for me to get my exams from there. He wanted you to go too." Alex and dad did get on. I remember he was desperate for me to have a friend, he reckoned I was too much of a loner, even though that was the way he was himself. He made our house a regular home-from-home for Alex.

No, I loved Alex, that's what kept us together. Perhaps he loved me more than I gave him credit for. Perhaps his back-to-front feeling of hatred for me later was genuine, not just expediency.

"I didn't want to go to that snob place," Alex says vehemently. "And don't tell me it wasn't."

I don't. I can feel his hand shaking with suppressed anger

on the gun behind my neck. I'd never guessed his resentment went that far back. Mine does too, beyond the bomb.

We're by Anna's place now. Alex steers me in with the barrel of his gun. I'm amazed to see the house appears in perfect condition. The upstairs windows have been repaired, the boards have been taken down from the frames. The lawn is cut, the drive free of weeds, the flower-beds are blooming.

"I keep it like this," Alex says. "Wait till you see inside."

"I thought you lived up in Bearwood," I say sharply.

"I do," he says. "I come up here once a week to make sure everything's in order." He's proud too of the good job he's made, glowing with satisfaction – which doesn't remove the problem of the gun. I try wriggling it away from my neck.

"Don't try any tricks!" he hisses. "This is no joke."

He makes me stand in the corner of the porch, face against the brick, hands on my head, while he unlocks the door. Then it's back to the gun under my ear as he marches me inside.

The house is shining new inside too, paintwork sparkles, fresh wallpaper. Weeks and weeks and weeks of labour have gone into this. I wonder whether the rest is the same.

But I'm not given a guided tour. We go straight into the front room. There's a three-piece suite and a television fixed up to a battery. I haven't seen a television working since we lived in the commune. Now's not the moment to ask if I can have a look. A piano. The room's immaculate. Not the kind of room in which you'd honestly want to spill blood.

Alex makes me sit on the settee. He's trembling again, very intense. It strikes me – here's a madman, and a mad man: I know all about my anger, thank you very much. Sometimes I sit whole days on end preventing myself from wrecking everything. And Anna feels sorry for me. I'd probably kill her if I gave way to it.

"She was mine," he says. "Anna. You took her away from me. That's what I can't forgive."

I protest. "When I 'took her away' you and Budge were trying to blast her house down. This house. She needed

106

protection. Anyway people aren't bits of property. You can't claim them just like that."

"I found her, two days before," he says. "On my own. Budge wasn't there. We talked. She let me in. We talked more. I won't go into details. I was going to come back for her. Budge found out. One of the others split on me – jealous sods. He messed it all up. If I'd got my hands on the gun I'd have shot him, not you."

My mind whirls. Surely it wasn't like that? Anna's always denied she met Alex the day before, or any other day. I rack my brains. I try to think. Wouldn't she have told me? She's told me everything, everything. Surely. She's so honest. She's no secrets. Even if I've told her nothing.

"It's true," he says. "Every bit of it. I don't suppose she's ever told you."

I shake my head. Then I think: there's no reason why she should have told me. It wasn't any business of mine, whether it's true or not. It might be true. If it is it doesn't matter. Except it's Alex and he still feels the special connection and the sight of me this morning has driven him crazy. And Anna, it's a funny time to think of her this way, but I'm not sure I love her, not enough to sacrifice myself for her. I think crazily, why be selfish? I've enjoyed her this long. Why not share her? "Your time's up, number one!" Or was I number two? She never said.

"Believe me," Alex says sincerely. "I've never lied to you."

I look at him. It's true as far as I know. Except all that was years ago and Alex is crazy and if he's trying to make me feel that Anna betrayed me it won't work.

"We were friends, and you pinched her," Alex insists.

No use talking about possessions and objects.

"If we were friends you had your chance to come away with me," I say. "Except you didn't take it. You stuck with Budge. And look what trouble that led to."

"Budge," he says. "I hated his guts. You did me a favour killing him. But he had a hold over me." For a moment I think I've got him on the run. What do they say about madmen – talk to them, get their confidence. But Alex is too far gone and I remember Alex was a pretty keen hunter when they chased me through the coppice. Oh no, he would have loved to get me like this then.

Suddenly he lifts the gun and as I cower shoots out the window. He shoots at everything in the room, there are bullets ricocheting all around. It's a miracle neither of us gets hit. The room is full of breaking glass.

"The bitch," he says. "She betrayed me. Bitches, they're all bitches. You're better off without them. Brothers, sisters, lovers, parents. I'd be doing you a favour."

He looks at me with a look in his eyes I can't fathom. Does he mean I'd be better off dead and out of it all? Or is it his way of wooing me back? He looks at me with the eye of a bomb. I wish I'd shot that fox.

POSTSCRIPT

Helicopter pilot Adrian Gravinski

Following instructions of the Tripartite Commission we delivered the following items approved by directive 51/97(d)/M8499, viz. two sheep, two goats, a coop of hens. All were landed safely by parachute in the field below the cottage at co-ordinates S25/W69 in the Affected Zone. The only person observed was a woman who came out of the cottage and stood and watched us. There appeared to be no other people in the vicinity although in the lane below the cottage a blue car was seen which appeared to have hit a tree and careered into the ditch. Whether or not this was a recent occurrence it was not possible to ascertain.

Also in this series

THE BEST LITTLE GIRL IN THE WORLD
Steven Levenkron

Francesca is five-feet four, pretty, slim and intelligent – at least that's how she appears to the rest of the world. But what she sees when she looks at her reflection is a fat, flabby, grotesque 'monster'. Suddenly, meals become dangerous to her. Food is the enemy and must be beaten! And what starts as determination soon becomes a frightening obsession – anorexia nervosa – with everyone realizing that her life is in danger . . .

THE DAY THEY CAME TO ARREST THE BOOK
Nat Hentoff

Whoever heard of a literary classic being banned from school? Well, that's just what happens at the George Mason High School, when a small group of parents and students brand *Huckleberry Finn* as racist, sexist and immoral, and persuade the principal to remove it from the library shelves. There is plenty to agree and disagree with in this provocative and witty portrait of a community in conflict.

LOCKED IN TIME
Lois Duncan

When seventeen-year-old Nore Robbins arrives at the old Louisiana plantation home of her father and his new wife, she is prepared for unhappiness. She did not expect her new family to be so *different*, nor can she understand her own mixed-up feelings about them. As time passes she pieces together a strange and terrible truth about the family; Nore alone is a threat to their secret – and threats must be destroyed.